Chasing Sunrise

Chasing Sunrise

EMILY MAH

Emily Mah

ISBN 978-1-7339154-0-3

Library of Congress Control Number: 2019939704

Cover & interior designed and formatted by:

www.emtippettsbookdesigns.com

For Sarah, Jordan, and Danielle
Champions, warriors, and people I'd never be able to flee from on
foot. I'm grateful our family's not like that.

1

I sat on a patch of dead grass beside Aunt Cassie's house as the sun rose. My skin already tingled as if I'd rubbed it with heat cream. Even though it was winter and the temperature below freezing, my jacket lay on the ground behind me, leaving my arms bare. With a deep breath of clean, chilled air, I braced myself for the full force of the oncoming pain.

The desert around me was quiet, and I was glad for that. It seemed that every animal I could think of that lived out here was poisonous in some way. Scorpions, rattlesnakes, various types of spiders––and I wasn't an outdoorsy person to begin with. I found myself taken in by the stillness of it all, though. There were no birds chirping, or leaves rustling in the wind, no distant sound of cars whooshing down the road, or buzz of an errant porch light attracting insects.

There was just the broad, flat Taos Valley with its deep, jagged line of canyon in the distance, and beyond that were the mountains, their sharp angles softened with a layer of evergreen trees. Now the sky was turning a deep, vivid pink with wispy clouds looking like they'd caught fire.

I felt more than saw the sunrise. One moment my skin burned with an annoying tingle, and the next it felt like I was laid out atop a hot griddle with molten metal poured over me. I was certain that my flesh was being incinerated this time, but I'd thought that last time and the time before. Clenching my teeth and holding my breath, I waited for the sensation to break. It had before, so it had to this time. Still I gripped my small gold cross pendant and prayed to any deity who would listen. I begged, mentally, for forgiveness for my weakness. *Please, give me another chance, another day.*

Tears leaked from my eyes, and that was the first sign I had that the pain was abating. Their cool tracks down my cheeks quenched the fire and that sensation spread across my face and down over the rest of my body.

And then it was all over, the external pain at least. It was just me, the silent desert, and the yawning chasm of emptiness I felt inside. Tears didn't ease that pain though. It was bottomless.

I pulled on my jacket, got to my feet, and took a good, long look at my aunt's house. It was, she told me, an "Earthship" and was made from all recycled materials. The walls were made from stacked used tires and rammed earth... or something like that. At least her weirdness was a distraction from an otherwise bleak life.

WHEN I WALKED into the kitchen, Aunt Cassie blinked at me, as if surprised I was still there.

Which made sense. My arrival last night was the first time we'd seen each other since I was a baby. She and my recently murdered father hadn't been close.

Dad had always called her a kook, and the description fit. She had her hair up in two bunches, like a six-year-old might wear it, and her lean frame was engulfed in an enormous bathrobe that was faded in splotches, as if someone had poured bleach on it while it was crumpled on the floor. Ratty old flip-flops that looked like they'd been fished up out of a dumpster adorned her feet. Basically, she looked like you'd expect the owner of this Earthship house to look.

"Did you go out for a walk?" she asked.

"I wanted to watch the sunrise."

She gestured around the bizarre structure she lived in. "You can see the sunrise just fine from in here. The house is heated with passive solar, you know?"

I looked at the south wall of windows. My room had an east facing window, so my aunt was not wrong that there was plenty of sunlight inside this house. Surely she understood why I'd wanted a break from this place, though...

Where we stood was a loft that included the kitchen and the bedroom where I'd slept (the main and, as far as I could tell, only entrance to the house was on the second floor because this thing was built into the side of a hill.) Downstairs was the room that Aunt Cassie used as her studio, and her bedroom was off that, a misshapen bump that jutted out from the otherwise boxy structure. My bedroom was a misshapen bump inside the structure, like a little cancerous growth anchored to the kitchen wall.

Downstairs, just inside the wall of windows, was a giant planter that was the size of an outside flower bed. In it grew banana trees and a million other random plants I didn't recognize, and they made the whole place smell like a greenhouse. The only power supplies to the house were a set of solar panels on the roof and a propane tank. All water was from cisterns fed by rain.

If that sounds weird, trust me, I'm only getting started describing this place. The interior walls were made of a mix of concrete and recycled bottles, which had been stacked kind of like bricks with the concrete mortared around them. To me, this made it look like the place had some crazy disease, a pox of some sort. The brown, green, white, and blue bottles had been arranged in swirls and whirls that were probably meant to look fancy, but to me the overall effect said, "set of a low-budget science fiction movie."

The kitchen counters were made out of concrete, and I don't mean the fancy concrete that trendy interior designers favor. These were gritty and you could still see the trowel marks, making it a porous surface used for food preparation–a microbiologist's dream and a kitchen inspector's worst nightmare. The sink was a blobby depression with a drain at the bottom.

Oh, and there was the waterfall. Even now as I stood looking at my aunt, rainwater from the cisterns ran down the inside of the north wall behind me, tumbling over river rock that had been stuck into the concrete wall with far less care than the empty bottles. The water plunged on down through a hole in the floor to the downstairs, where it pooled in a low pond, like a koi pond without koi. There the water waited to be pumped back up again. This, my aunt explained, aerated it. I didn't dare ask if it was treated beyond that, and tried not to think of all the bird poop and other stuff that could accumulate on her roof, only to be washed into the water system by rain. Because the downstairs pond's lip was almost flush with the floor, it probably collected dust bunnies and other dirt too.

Aunt Cassie lifted an eyebrow, signalling that it was my turn to talk. What had she last said? Oh yes, she wanted to know why I'd gone outside for the sunrise, rather than watching from my room. "I had trouble sleeping. I wanted some fresh air. I didn't go far." All of that was true, especially the part about me not sleeping well last night. I hadn't slept well any night since my father's murder. How could I? Dad and I hadn't been super close, with me away at boarding school in the winter and camp in the summer, but he'd always been there for me. Whenever I'd needed anything, he was just a phone call away.

Now if I dialed his phone, I'd get voicemail, and no call back five minutes later. I'd cried most of the three-day bus trip to Taos but that hadn't taken the edge off the pain. Life had become this nightmare I couldn't wake up from. I wasn't going to jolt back to a world with my dad in it, and that thought kept running circles in my mind, like a dog chasing its tail.

I went towards the coffeemaker, but my aunt blocked me and pointed at the toaster. "I've got Pop Tarts."

"Okay. Can I drink coffee with my Pop Tarts?"

"It's not good for you." She grabbed the carafe out of the coffeemaker and poured all the contents into her cup. Well, bowl, actually. She was drinking coffee out of a bowl as if it was miso soup.

There were a few logical arguments I could have made about the relative health benefits of Pop Tarts versus coffee, but I figured it was best not to antagonize the one family member I had left in the world.

It took a little digging in the pantry (built from scrap wood set unevenly in the concrete wall) to find the ancient, faded box of Pop Tarts. Disturbingly, the tarts themselves looked the same as any others I'd ever seen. I dropped them in the toaster and rooted through the strange little propane power fridge for something to drink other than the rainwater that was pouring through the room right then. The best I could find was a shot of probiotic yogurt shoved all the way in the back. I drank that and snagged my Pop Tarts once they were ready.

On my way past the open door to my room, I caught sight of myself in the full-length mirror on the far wall and stopped to stare. My medium-brown hair had always been mousy, and the perfect mix of wavy and straight to look disheveled at all times. Stylists told me I needed to either straighten it or mousse it to preserve the curls, but I'd opted for a mix of ponytails and not caring instead.

Now my hair was glossy and straight, save for the lift at the roots that made it look like I was wearing product.

My body used to be frumpy and dumpy, fat that I could no longer claim was baby fat making my stomach and butt slouch. Now I looked like I spent twenty hours a week working out. My thighs were slim and my legs looked longer, although I had measured myself to ascertain that I hadn't gained any height.

I suppose most girls would look at a transformation like this as a godsend, but it filled me with both confusion and disappointment. I took a defiant bite of Pop Tart, then wondered if it was supposed to be so chewy. Perhaps these things really did go stale. Sugary flavor coated the inside of my mouth and my intestines writhed in protest. I forced myself to swallow, then went to look over the banister to the studio below.

By now, Aunt Cassie was seated there, crushing what looked like herbs with a mortar and pestle. Around her, hanging on racks, was dyed wool that she would later spin into yarn.

As if feeling my gaze, she looked up. "So school starts at eight. You can borrow my car for the first day. Then they'll set you up with the bus and all that."

"Thank you... that's generous."

She shrugged and resumed grinding herbs, pausing to look up again when I didn't move away from the banister. "Something wrong?"

"I don't know how to drive," I confessed. I was seventeen for a few more days, and New York only allowed people my age to get junior licenses. It wasn't like here in New Mexico where I'd seen people looking fifteen or so behind the wheel.

Which my aunt seemed to remember as she laid the mortar and pestle aside. "Sorry, I should have thought of that."

"No. I'm sorry to be a burden."

"You aren't a burden, Liana. You're family." She came marching up the stairs. "We'll get you enrolled in driver's ed as soon as the Southampton police say it's okay, though, all right?"

"Sure, yeah." This subdivision she lived in was so far from town, and the houses so far apart, I would definitely need a car, even if the thought of driving one was daunting. The police department back home had asked me to stay off the radar and not do things like get a driver's license or access my bank account, but I had to believe that wouldn't be forever.

"Come on." She grabbed her car keys off a hook by the front door.

HALF AN HOUR later I sat in the office of Taos High School, marveling at how it was a normal public school, just like I'd seen on TV. It had a bell that rang, lockers that clanged, and no one wearing their pajamas to class. That was one luxury of boarding school, though, the ability to be that slovenly.

Fluorescent lights buzzed overhead while the secretary tapped away at the keyboard of her computer.

Students streamed past in the hallways, some of them–guys mostly–pausing to peer in at me. My first instinct was to hunch my shoulders and pull into myself. I wasn't used to guys looking twice at me. I was comfortable as the nerdy invisible girl who was always in the library studying on a Friday night. Several even waved at me with shy flips of their wrists before they moved out of sight. Bizarre.

The average complexions here were quite a bit darker than I was used to, and I could hear snippets of Spanish bouncing off the tile floors and cinder block walls.

A guy moseyed past the door and paused to look in. Blond hair, pale blue eyes, and skin with that ethereal, translucent quality that I'd seen girls try to mimic with countless cosmetic products. Normally I'd just gaze at a guy like him for as long as possible, then avert my eyes before he saw me staring. Being ordinary meant being beneath most guys' notice.

Now, though, had my transformation made it okay for me to get caught staring at him? Would I be like those girls in the television shows about public high schools I'd watched? The ones where the main character could turn the head of the hottest jock with their mix of good looks and new-girl mystique?

I wasn't brave enough to test it, nor was I quick enough to look away. Our gazes met, and his eyes widened a notch. A second later, he was gone, though I didn't remember seeing him step away. It was as if he'd winked out of existence. Well, that had gone about as well as I'd expected, truly.

"Liana Linacre?" the secretary called out.

"Yes." I slipped out of my seat and stepped up to the counter.

"We're doing the best we can with your schedule, but we don't have classics here."

"Sure," I said. "I know. Just whatever you can approximate." I really didn't want to step on any toes. The fewer people who noticed me here, the better. The police had suggested that I just do home study to finish out my senior year, but my old prep school said no way no how, not even considering my situation. Not even considering that I had already gotten early acceptance into Princeton, or that if I ditched every class from here on and missed the tests, I'd still probably pass with a B average.

My old school said that if I did my best to complete my coursework at another accredited high school, they'd work with me to issue a diploma on their fancy lambskin and name me valedictorian. I also suspected that if I tried independent study, I'd just fall into a deep funk and end up sleeping twenty hours a day. Guilt weighed on me like a mass of welded anvils and going through the motions of normal life was at least a distraction.

The secretary stared at my record. "May I ask why you're here, when you had a four-point-four average at this... uh... Hawke Academy? Sounds fancy. Is that a boarding school?"

"Yeah. It is. I'm here because my father passed away very suddenly."

Great, now my voice was wavering. I shut my eyes as they began to burn. *Don't cry, don't cry,* I ordered myself.

"Oh... sweetie, I'm sorry." The secretary laid a warm, dry palm on my hand. "I shouldn't have pried. You okay?"

I nodded, took a deep, shaky breath, and opened my eyes. The world wasn't too blurry. A few blinks cleared it up.

The secretary handed me a tissue and I pressed it to the inner corners of my eyes to sop up the tears before they escaped down my cheeks.

"Okay, so we don't have Latin either," she said. "Do you know any other foreign language?"

"Can I take Spanish?" I suggested. It sounded like a language that was useful around here, and I already had my three years of foreign language that the Ivy League required.

"Do you know any? It's too late in the year to start from scratch."

That was a point. I might be in mourning and desperate for a distraction, but that didn't make me superhuman. Besides, it occurred to me that in a school with so many Spanish speakers, people taking Spanish might be able to learn faster than I was used to at the Hawke Academy. "Right," I said. "I don't really need a foreign language."

"Do you want to take art?"

I hadn't done art in at least six years. "Sure." I had my reservations about that too, though. According to Wikipedia, Taos had started out as an artists' colony and was still inhabited by way more artists per capita than most cities of its size. But a challenge meant a distraction, so I was game.

"Okay, here you go." She grabbed a sheet of paper from the printer and handed it to me. "Here's a map of the school… except Corban's here and he's got your same homeroom. Corban, could you show Liana the way?"

I turned around and found myself toe-to-toe with the hot blond guy. He hadn't run away after all, and he was staring at me like he was looking at a ghost.

"Sure, Ms. Benitez," he said. He had his hands stuffed into the pockets of his sweatshirt and indicated with a jerk of his head that I was to follow him.

I hoisted my backpack to my shoulder and stepped out of the office into the crowded hallway. No sooner had I gotten my bearings than I found myself backed against a wall, Corban looking me straight in the eye.

"Listen," he said. "You can try to hide, but I know what you are. You're not welcome here."

2

I opened my mouth, but no sound came out. The halls were emptying, so the buzzing of the fluorescent lights overhead and a few giggles, whispers, and shoes squeaking on tile were soon the only sounds.

His expression grew quizzical. "And you can drop the act," he pressed, leaning forward so that he towered over me.

I held up my hands to defend myself, and he flinched back like I'd thrown a punch. As if I were a six-foot-tall jock, with perfect aim and a well-muscled arm. Given how broad Corban's shoulders were, I knew he could beat me to a pulp with one hand, so why was he so freaked?

Slowly he rounded to look at me again.

I still had my hands up. "I…" It came out as a squeak.

He looked me up and down, then shook his head. "Something doesn't add up here. Is this some kind of trick?"

I wasn't sure what "this" referred to, and my throat was no less dry nor more able to produce words than it had been seconds ago.

His gaze went from mildly baffled to utterly confused.

At least he stopped looming over me.

I took a deep, slow breath. "I just want to go to class," I said in a voice so soft it was barely more than a whisper.

He smirked at that, as if I'd told a joke. Then after a moment he said, "You're kidding, right? You think I'm going to let you go to class and mingle and make new friends?"

I couldn't tell if he was being ironic. It wasn't as if I was going to be a social butterfly, or even graceful enough to make one friend, let alone friends, plural. Did he know that, and was he mocking me? Or did my new appearance make me look socially ept?

The metallic rattle of a bell made me almost jump out of my skin.

Corban looked at me as if I were growing a second head right before his eyes. He folded his arms with the easy air of someone who knew he was where he belonged.

I wondered if I'd feel that way anywhere ever again. Home was the one place I'd felt I'd belonged and Dad was the one person who always loved me no matter what. Without him, I had no refuge anymore.

Great, my eyes were burning again. *Way to go, Liana. Cry in the hallway on your first day.*

"Stop it," Corban ordered. "I'm not in the mood for stupid tricks."

Indifference I could handle, but cruelty? Being told that my tears were a stupid trick?

My eyes flooded and I could feel my face scrunching up into a full-on ugly cry. I didn't know whether to be mortified, heartbroken, or just plain desperate to be elsewhere. What resulted was a combination of all three, an emotion that somehow managed to feel ten times worse than any one of them taken alone.

I thought life had been hard as a plain-Jane nobody at the Hawke Academy. That was naive.

The sound of a door swinging shut caused me to turn my head, and through the blur of my tears I could just make out the sign with the little, flat, skirt-clad figure that signalled the girls' restroom. As fast as my feet would carry me, I bolted for it, barrelled on through, and made my way somehow to a stall. Only when I felt the cool metal of its door against my palms and knew for certain that I was holding it shut, walling the world out, did I let the tears fall. I fumbled with the latch until I made it lock, then leaned against the cold tile wall and sobbed.

UTTER QUIET HAD descended. Everyone was in class, and here I was, hyperventilating and leaning against a wall that seeped the warmth out of me. I'd managed to get the tears to stop, but only just. I had to get control, and then perhaps I could leave school and hope that my aunt would take pity on me. I had just lost my father, her brother. She might understand.

Or she might snap something random at me, like that I had to eat more Pop Tarts, and then stalk off to do something like rehearse an opera solo. Not that I'd heard her singing. It just seemed like the type of thing she'd do, something loud and confident and utterly bizarre. She was more than I could take. Why couldn't I have a quiet, wool-spinning aunt with gray hair and a gentle voice? Why did my world have to be so full of people who poked and prodded me so far outside of my comfort zone at a time like this? Or I suppose it was more accurate to wonder why my world had to be so *empty*, except for someone like my aunt at a time like this.

And why did the first person I met at school have to be a dreamboat who was also a bully and a control freak? I'd had enough of those for one lifetime. Or maybe I was developing mental issues? Maybe Corban and Aunt Cassie were perfectly normal people and I merely misheard them and did crazed things as a result. Maybe Aunt Cassie had offered me oatmeal before I dove for the pantry, intent on finding ten-year-old Pop Tarts.

The door swung open, followed by the sound of footsteps. They paced slowly across the tile floor towards my stall.

I held my breath, as if this would make any difference. A glance under the door would show my feet. A peer through the crack would show the dark shape of me, cowering against the wall.

"So…" came Corban's voice. "You're not faking, are you?"

"What?" I squeaked. He'd followed me into the bathroom? He wasn't just a bully, he was a psychopath. Now he'd cornered me alone. My heart thudded with panic and I fumbled for my phone, only to have it slip through my fingers, hit the floor, and slide under the metal divider, into the next stall. I breathed a silent curse.

Corban's steps shifted and a moment later I heard him pick up my phone.

I shut my eyes and gripped my cross pendant, again pleading to any deity that might have a spare moment to save me. Was he about to kill me? Rape me? Why oh why had I screwed my life up so bad that even the Christian God might avert his eyes? Well, I had no one but myself to blame for that.

The phone beeped as Corban unlocked it.

How had he done that? The phone was keyed to my fingerprint. My chest muscles were so sore from hyperventilating that now I just held my breath and closed my eyes.

"Huh," he said. "Your only contact in here is a relative? Aunt Cassie?"

I wanted to scream, "What do you want?" but I couldn't. I kept my eyes screwed shut instead as more tears escaped down my cheeks.

"You show up here with a brand-new phone and no contacts. What are you running from?"

The police had recommended I replace my phone and not give out the number to anyone but my aunt and the family attorney, since whoever had killed my dad might come after me. Since no one had any idea who had killed him, I had no idea what I was running from.

Well, not no idea. I had guesses, but nothing more, and my guesses were all insane. Every time I went through them, guilt, that mass of welded anvils, pressed down even harder.

Corban walked over to stand on the other side of the door to my stall, paused a moment, then sighed. "Here." He squatted down and put my phone on the floor, then pushed it into my stall.

I slid down to sit on the cold, hard floor, snatched my phone up, and clutched it in my hand. My muscles were too tense for me to do anything more. If I had to dial 911, I probably wouldn't be able to. Much as I wanted to be a strong woman, I was far better at researching great solutions than I was at executing them. If I could read or study my way out of a situation, I was unstoppable.

That wouldn't work here.

Corban stood up again and I had the sense that he was staring at my door, or down at me through the door. "You're terrified, aren't you?" He didn't say it in a taunting way. On the contrary, he sounded confused.

Because he didn't think making threats and following me into the bathroom was frightening?

"And the grief thing," he added. "That's real, isn't it?"

"Can you please just go away?"

"I can't, no. I'm sure you can understand why."

I understood absolutely nothing about this current situation.

"Liana?"

"No," I breathed. "I don't understand."

For a long moment he said nothing, and the room was silent save for the sound of water dripping in one of the sinks.

Then he chuckled. "Um…" he began.

"Go away!" I managed to shriek, in a pitchy, mangled tone.

"So you do have a voice."

I hadn't put even a scratch in his resolve, and there was no sound to indicate that anyone outside the bathroom had heard me and was running to my rescue. I pulled my knees to my chest and shut my eyes like a little girl playing hide-and-seek, believing that if I couldn't see anyone else, they couldn't see me either. My hyperventilating was back and the shuddering sound of my gasps echoed off the metal walls of the stall.

I focused on making myself breathe the cold, fetid air–now that I was sitting on the floor, the air positively stank. Still, I breathed it. This situation was bad enough without me passing out.

Outside the stall, I heard Corban sigh again, then the soft sound of him sitting down as well. With the metal door dividing us, we both leaned against the tile wall.

And inexplicably, I began to feel better.

"Yeah, this is real pain, all right," he said.

The pain was leaving me, as if Corban were draining it from my body.

Yeah, I'd gone completely wacko now. I imagined someone having to explain how they found me in the girl's bathroom on my first day at a new school, pummelling a guy with my fists and shouting at him to give me back my pain. When I thought he might hurt me, I'd been too terrified to act, but the very idea that anyone or anything might tamper with my grief from my father's death was enough to make me want to punch him, hard.

And just like that, the hurt was back, that sharp pang in my chest every time I breathed, that pressure behind my eyes of tears ready to leak at any second. It was excruciating, but I cherished it. I luxuriated in it. It was all I had left of my father, and no matter how it burned, I needed it. The depth of the void left behind was my reminder of how much he'd loved me. Despite all my flaws, someone really had loved me once.

"Yeah," said Corban. "Something's not adding up."

"Please leave," I begged.

"So, I can tell that you're dealing with a lot, here. I don't mean to pile on or anything but… you do know that you're a vampire, right?"

3

"**V**ampire." The word hung between us, like a dull note struck on a piano that rang in the air, overstaying its welcome. My heart broke. Was I really? More tears flooded my eyes and I began to cry in earnest.

"I mean," he went on, "you are and you aren't. You've got human emotions, which like I said, doesn't add up."

I wrapped my arms more firmly around my knees and settled my backpack against my side. The soles of my boots scraped against the tile as I shifted my weight.

"Okay, look," said Corban. "I do not want to be causing you pain, here. I just… I hunt vampires and I thought you were one and we can't have any running around this school. You can understand that, right? A no-bloodsucker policy?"

"You believe in vampires?" I asked.

"You and I both know they exist, so let's not dance around that whole issue," he said. "Are you some new breed? Have vamps evolved new skills?"

It occurred to me if I called 911 from my phone now, this could be over. Any dispatcher who overheard what Corban said would think he was nuts.

I didn't do that, though, because I was still frozen, and I suspected he *wasn't* nuts. He was only the second person I'd ever met who talked about vampires being real. Being one of the select few to know about them had been its own little prison sentence for me, so isolating that I'd begun to doubt my memories, despite the evidence I saw in the mirror every morning.

"What do you know about vampires?" I whispered, my lack of voice so breathy, I wondered if he'd even hear.

"I know they're demons who take the bodies of humans, and they spread through a population like a virus. That's why I kill them."

"So you're going to kill me?" I asked.

For a moment, he said nothing. Then, "Do you want a vampire loose in this high school? Be completely honest."

I wiped my eyes on the back of my hand. "No," I said. "I don't."

"Interesting. So, would you agree with me that if you are one, you need to be taken care of?"

"I don't want to die."

"Sure, nobody does. That's a really un-vampy answer, though. Usually it's some screed about how they're the superior race and they can feed on whoever they want and no one can defeat them and all that."

So I wasn't just a vampire, I was also doing it wrong. Great.

"Hey," he said. "That was a compliment."

"Still hung up on the you-killing-me thing," I said.

"Oh… Yeah, that's fair. You seem human, though. Either you're in line for an Academy Award, or you're not acting."

I would never, in a million years, win an Academy Award.

"Tell me what happened to you," he said. "Help me understand what you are. Did someone turn you or… what?"

Those weren't memories I wanted to revisit, especially not to share with a stranger, still, if I had to argue my case, I needed to order my thoughts.

THE HAWKE ACADEMY was a wealthy campus of stone buildings that sent dreaming spires skyward along its rooflines. The doorways and windows topped out in gothic arches. There was a main quad with all the academic buildings and dining hall, and then our dorms were down a hill, abutting miles and miles of state-owned forest land, so remote that we could hear the crack of hunting rifles during deer season. It was the kind of place that evoked a sense of isolation, and everyone there had been in mourning since last fall.

It was strange to remember the old pain that I'd felt when one of the most popular girls, Rachel, had committed suicide. That hurt seemed so pale and distant now, but had been vivid and raw then. I hadn't known her well, but she'd lived in my dorm and my roommate had elected to move in with her old roommate. This left me with a room to myself on the first floor with windows facing the dark and silent woods.

Then over Christmas break, another student from a different dorm disappeared. I'd known Evan slightly better, since our fathers were friends. The loss of two students in three months had hit everyone like a volcanic eruption followed by a shattering earthquake, and I endured this alone.

The rest of the school knit together, united by the pain. The girls in my house spent hours in the dayroom crying, sipping cocoa and coffee, braiding each others' hair, and spinning a cocoon of warmth and comfort that did not include me.

Though if you'd asked them, they'd have blamed me for this. I was standoffish, a snob. I didn't dedicate enough time to basic makeup techniques, or overcoming my terminal lack of fashion sense. It was my decision to spend every afternoon and evening in the library, studying, then head straight back to my dorm room without speaking to anyone. It was my decision to eat my meals alone. The cycle of isolation, causing the others to close ranks without me, thus feeding more isolation, had been going on for years at this point. I had no idea how to end it. Simply setting out to make friends wasn't possible in such a small community. I couldn't decide to become a new girl who people would be curious about. I was old news that no one cared to revisit.

On the night that began like so many before but ended quite differently, I lay in the dark after lights-out with my stomach roiling and pointless, stressful thoughts babbling away in my mind. When someone tapped at the window, I'd just about jumped out of my skin. Surely it was an intruder, a murderer.

It couldn't be just some guy, enticed by a girl with a room to herself.

When the tap came the second time, I sat up and saw, much to my horror, a dark shadow outlined in the moonlight. In upstate New York, the world was blanketed with snow all winter, and that reflected plenty of moonlight for me to see this shadow by. It was unmistakably human.

"Liana?" came a plaintive voice. "It's me. Evan. You in there?"

"Evan?" I asked.

"Yeah. Can you open the window?"

I bounded up from my bed and unlatched it. "You're alive! Are you okay? Quick, come in."

He'd climbed awkwardly into the room along with a blast of cold air, and I could see that he wasn't well. His clothes hung loose on his body and his face was gaunt and his skin bone white. "Shhh," he'd said. "You can't tell anyone I'm here, okay?"

"Everyone's worried sick about you. Your dad hired a detective. You don't answer your cell phone. Where have you been?" I pulled the window closed and twisted the latch shut.

"It's a kind of long story and I need you to hear me out." In the darkness, his eyes seemed enormous in his hollow face. His look of furtive desperation shut me up and made me sit down on my bed and draw my comforter around me.

This was already the longest conversation I'd ever had with him. Our dads being friends had meant that every now and then we travelled to school together (with him wearing headphones the entire time and pretending I didn't exist), but we hadn't even done that for a couple of years.

So that moment, when he'd sat down on the bed opposite me, was surreal for all kinds of reasons.

"Are you in trouble?" I asked.

"More trouble than you can imagine."

I didn't doubt this for a moment. Evan had been a popular guy, the kind who played football and considered a steady girlfriend an encumbrance. Even the most stylish, beautiful girls in the school accepted his terms of dating when he felt like it, but not settling on anyone in particular.

There were plenty of bedroom windows the old Evan could have climbed into. This new Evan who sat across from me was a mere shadow in comparison. Whatever had happened to him, it was serious.

I assumed it was drugs, or perhaps he'd been kidnapped and held hostage and starved. But since he was safe now, I figured I'd listen to his story and then we'd tell the dorm warden he was here and his dad would come up from Southampton and everyone would have a joy-fest, knowing he was all right.

For a long moment he didn't say anything, just looked down at his slim, bony hands. I noticed that a coldness emanated from him, and a scent that reminded me of midnight in a graveyard.

"I, um, I hooked up with someone over break," he began.

I nodded. Maybe he'd gotten involved with some crazy stalker who'd driven him out of his home. Maybe she was part of some kind of cult.

"And, she bit me while we were… you know."

My thoughts slowed and stopped, and I lifted an eyebrow. Given the magnitude of what had happened with him going missing for weeks, this seemed like a trivial detail, and I couldn't fathom why he shared it with me. Also, my lack of any real friendship with Evan meant it was extra weird to have him tell me about his doing "you know." There was little point in mentioning that I did not know, not from personal experience. I'd never even kissed anyone.

He shut his eyes for a long moment. "She said she was a vampire."

Yeah, okay, I thought. *He fell in with a cult.* They'd starved him and possibly had him locked up somewhere. That explained his ravenous look and his fear of getting help, but I was still relieved. He was safe now, and I'd get him help once I got him to calm down a little more. I was *happy* in that moment. Evan was safe and back and the school would have something to celebrate.

"And she had me bite her and drink her blood."

"Gross, Evan," I said, then shut my mouth. The last thing he needed was judgment, even though what he'd said was, indeed, gross. "Sorry."

He shook his head, dismissing my criticism. "It's fine. The thing is, I think she was telling the truth."

"Evan–"

"No, listen to me. I can't go out in the daytime. The sunlight burns me like I've stepped into a stream of hot lava. I can't get into my house. I try and it's like I hit a solid wall of air, and I'm starving. I've tried eating food and even drinking animal blood and… I'm so hungry. Right now, the smell of you." He inhaled like he might be able to get high just snorting air. "I can sense your pulse. I can feel the heat of your blood. Please, Lia. I don't want to just feed on some random stranger. Help me."

Well, I reacted about as well as one would expect, which is to say that I first tried not to laugh, then when I realized he was serious, I was grossed out. I wanted to get the dorm warden, but when I moved towards the door Evan moved like a shot, blocking my way, grabbing my wrists and begging me, cajoling me.

"Please," he'd said, his fingers digging into my wrists. "I just need to feed once. I need to know if this is for real, and I need to not feel so hungry. I promise you, it'll just be once."

I put forth all the logical reasons why this was a bad idea, such as: Was he out of his mind? Did he really think I'd let him drink my blood? Was this some kind of sick prank? If it weren't for his emaciated body, I'd have believed that the rest of the dorm was filming this and would project it on the wall of the dining hall the next night.

But he begged and pleaded and put his arms around me, pressing his cold body against mine. This was more contact than I'd ever had with any guy, and Evan, even in his starved state, was still plenty attractive. His cold-stone scent had suffused me as he pressed me back onto my bed and dug his teeth into the side of my neck.

4

Back in the bathroom of Taos High School, my joints had grown stiff from sitting curled up on a cold tile floor. I stared off into space as my traitorous memory called up the intensely erotic sensation of lying on a bed with Evan's body wrapped around mine. I recalled hearing his soft gulps as he drank my blood, while his hands caressed my shoulders and down my sides. He had even tried to slip them under the ratty t-shirt I'd worn to bed, but I'd squirmed at that.

He'd drunk deep that night, stopping only when my vision began to go gray and I implored him to quit. Then he started to panic, apologizing and begging me to be all right.

"Liana?" said Corban. His voice was calm and patient, like that of an old friend, someone who knew my quirks and liked me anyway.

But he wasn't an old friend. He was a vampire killer, and therefore my enemy. Right? Or was he my ally because he could have prevented this from happening to me if he'd killed Evan two weeks ago?

"Isn't killing vampires murder?" I whispered. Then I clamped my mouth shut. Why, even in my supernaturally altered state, couldn't I stop being such a dork? This guy had threatened to kill me and the first question I had was about the legal ramifications.

He went with it, though. "Vampires are already dead, technically. That's something else about you, you're breathing and I'm guessing you have a regular body temperature and a pulse. Which also doesn't add up."

"They're dead?"

"Yeah. They're a form of demon that inhabits a human body after the soul leaves. They can do a very convincing impression of the person they stole the body from sometimes, because they have the person's memories, but they aren't the same individual."

"But… do they know that?" I was still myself, as far as I was aware. I wasn't a demon, I didn't think.

"I have no idea if they know. Maybe, maybe not. The person who did this to you was a friend, I take it?"

Hardly. I got some toilet paper and blew my nose. "No," I managed to whisper.

"Did he try to be more than a friend?"

"Yeah."

My mind cast itself back to the sensation of Evan slipping his hands under my shirt for the first time, and the feel of his skin on mine. That was the instant when I understood how girls who vowed to stay virgins got pregnant, because if Evan had wanted more any night that he'd fed, I don't know if I would have stopped him. I would have just really, really regretted it the next day.

And then there was the first time he'd fitted his mouth to mine and kissed me, conveying that I wasn't just a food source to him. He didn't just need me. He wanted me and I wanted him.

I remembered lying breathless as his kisses trailed down my neck and his hands worked their magic on my bare skin.

"Liana," Corban cut in. "Did you hear what I asked?"

"No…"

The reproving tone of his voice called back memories of guilty mornings after, when I tied a scarf around my neck to hide bite marks and hunched over my plate in the dining hall, shovelling down red meat and dark, leafy greens while people still gossiped about whether or not Evan was dead. I was reminded of all those days when I was too chicken to spill my secret and all the times that I vowed to end things with him, but weeks rolled by and I never did.

It called back memories of me staring at myself in the mirror, hating the pale-skinned, anemic person I saw as I told myself over and over again that Evan was using me. He was making me do exactly what he wanted and literally bleeding me dry. Logic solved all my homework problems. Why couldn't it solve this one for me?

It called back memories of the intense shame I felt every time I let him in my window. While I'd been the antisocial nobody, I could cling to the belief that I was a strong, independent woman. Evan had proven me wrong, though. I was every bit as needy and pliable as the shallow, boy-crazy girls I'd always looked down on. The only difference had been my lack of opportunities.

Corban shifted his weight and angled his body so that I could see one blue eye in the crack at the edge of the metal stall, where the brackets bolted it to the tile. If I could see his eye, he could see me.

I turned my face away, cheeks growing warm.

"Did you ever bite him?" he asked. "Drink his blood?"

My face grew hotter. I couldn't bring myself to answer that question.

"You've got some physical characteristics of a vampire," he said. "No offense, but your beauty isn't natural. And you kind of smell like a vampire, but only kind of. You actually smell like you're wearing clothes that were stored in a casket with a vampire. You, yourself, smell more human."

He shifted again and held out his cell phone, his reflection showing clearly on its dark screen. "Huh," he said. "You also have a reflection."

"Of course I do. If you can see me, I'm gonna also show up in a mirror. Being visible at all requires reflection of light in the visible spectrum. Light that bounces off me is gonna bounce off your cell phone screen."

"You showing off, nerd girl?" he asked, chuckling.

I buried my face against my knees.

"Because if you want to do a battle of the minds," he went on, "I surrender. I've never been the sharpest knife in the drawer. You know, it's the trade-off for looking as good as I do."

Whatever, I thought.

"Okay, sorry." He sounded contrite now, like we were on an awkward first date and he was worried he'd just blown it. "The thing is, I'm trying to figure out what you are. Can you walk in the sun?"

"Yeah," I whispered.

"You can? It doesn't burn?"

"Only at sunrise."

He didn't respond to that. I lifted my head and saw that he was gone, but before I could open the stall door and peer out, the bathroom door swung inward and at least two sets of boots clomped in.

"There is someone in here," said a feminine voice.

I froze, mortified, my shame ticking upward with every clomp as whoever this was walked towards me.

"Hey, are you Liana Linacre?" the voice asked.

How was I supposed to answer this girl's question? This was not how I wanted to meet people at my new school.

"Hey," said a second voice, a slightly deeper one. "I know your aunt. I heard about your dad. Mr. Martinez just wanted to make sure you didn't get lost."

I wiped my eyes with a scrap of toilet paper and got to my feet. With a deep, bracing breath, I opened the door and found myself face to face with two girls. One, the first who'd spoken, looked Latina and wore a high ponytail and had beautiful, elfin features. Her skin was a deep olive and her hair a shade of brown so dark that it was almost black. The other was shorter, stockier, and had darker skin and black hair that was so coarse that the shorter strands of her ponytail stuck out, rather than flowing down her back. I blinked at her, realizing I was looking at a real, live Native American, and not one like Mike Benoit at the Hawke Academy, a hazel-eyed blond who bragged about the scholarships he could get because he was legally registered with a tribe whose name he couldn't pronounce. Her bloodlines were much, much more concentrated. Her smile was broad and her eyes kind.

Both sets of eyes were kind. From the way they were dressed–jeans with knee boots and solid-colored, long-sleeve shirts–I suspected they were popular, but not the snooty kind of popular.

"Hi," I croaked.

"Hi," said the Latina girl. "I'm Gina. This is Amy. We're in your homeroom."

The Native girl gave me a shy wave.

"Yeah, sorry…" I said. "I was on my way there–"

"Don't worry about it," said Gina. "You're fine. Are you ready to come to class? Or if you still need a while, we can take you to the nurse's office. She's cool about letting you stay there until you feel better."

The nurse at the Hawke Academy ruled her domain with an iron fist. You did not enter without fever over a hundred, and you left the moment she said you were well. She rarely wrote notes excusing people from class or sports activities. Every year we had a nasty outbreak of flu or norovirus or both because of her draconian policies, and there were usually two or three students who left the school over it.

"Th-thanks. Um. How bad do I look?" I gestured at my cheeks.

"You look fine," said Gina with a shrug.

"No tearstains?"

"Nuh-uh," she said. "You didn't cry very hard. I can tell."

"Um…" I'd sobbed my eyes out. I also wanted to ask them about Corban, but I wasn't sure what to ask. "Did you know there's a vampire hunter on campus?" wasn't a good way to broach the subject. Besides, it was only ever in my imagination that I knew the right things to say to get what I needed. This was real life, so I did what I always did in real life, I chickened out. "I'm okay. Yeah, I can go to class."

The two girls parted and I walked out of the stall and over to the mirror. Sure enough, my cheeks weren't puffy. My eyes weren't even red-rimmed and my lower lashes didn't have that clumped look they usually got after I cried. I wondered if this was another vampire power, but that begged the question of whether or not I was a vampire.

Gina and Amy led me down the empty, echoing hallways to class, where I greeted the assembled students with a sheepish nod.

The room was a plain, utilitarian space with a whiteboard on one wall and lockers on another. The air smelled like incense–which was verboten on the Hawke Academy campus–and the teacher wore a bolo tie, black shirt and a belt with a giant, turquoise-encrusted buckle with his dark jeans and cowboy boots. His getup alone made me feel like I was in a movie with a character actor trying to evoke the look and feel of the Southwest.

He even spoke English with a slight Spanish accent as he welcomed me in and directed me to sit at a desk near the front.

There was a prompt for a writing assignment on the board, but Mr. Martinez put a laptop down in front of me. "This is your netbook," he explained. "Everyone in the school has one, and we need to get you set up in an account."

I blinked, surprised. The Hawke Academy did not provide computer hardware; rather it required that the students buy their own of a certain set of specs or above. Only the scholarship kids might also get money to cover a laptop. My old laptop was still back at the Hawke Academy, or perhaps it had been moved to my house. Our family lawyer would probably handle all that stuff; I didn't even know.

This netbook was cheap, I noted, probably not more than a couple hundred dollars, and had the school district name and logo etched into the plastic casing. In order to log into it, I first had to fill out form after form to create an account.

It was a good way to spend that first hour, because otherwise I think I would have gawked at everyone and everything in the room. I knew I had to get out of the habit of being amazed at how many Latinos there were, and at how New Mexico seemed like it borrowed half its styling from old Western movies. Intellectually I understood that it was the other way around.

Once I had my netbook working, I cast my gaze around the room once again.

"Looking for someone?" Mr. Martinez asked.

"Corban?" I asked. "He was supposed to bring me here this morning."

"Corban Alexander. Yes, he had to be excused. A family issue."

I wondered if his whole family were vampire hunters.

The bell rang and everyone scrambled to pack away their stuff. Gina appeared beside my desk and offered to show me to my next class. I thanked her and followed her bouncy ponytail out the door and into the crowded hall.

In the stream of students going the other way, I caught sight of Corban. A jolt shot through my heart; it was unmistakably him. He stood out like a strand of white cat fur on black jeans.

He met my gaze, and was gone.

And I was confused.

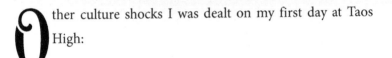

5

Other culture shocks I was dealt on my first day at Taos High:

- All of the lockers were in the homerooms, which is not how things ever were in the movies, which always
- showed them lining the halls. The thing was, there wasn't a lot to put in a locker these days because…
- The textbooks stayed in the classrooms. If we needed to use textbooks for homework, we had to check them out overnight.
- The school looked pretty generic, but the cafeteria had panoramic windows that showed the mountain skyline. And nobody seemed to find this remarkable.
- The cafeteria served enchiladas with glommy cheese and a spicy scent that tasted amazing, to

my palate at least. Everyone else dumped tons of salsa on theirs. Very, very hot salsa. New York "hot" was what New Mexico considered "mild"– bordering on bland, chunky ketchup.

- I was what New Mexicans called an "Anglo". Apparently that term applied to anyone who was neither Latino or Native American.

- The Latinos preferred to be called "Hispanic" and referred to themselves as "Spanish." To me they looked more Mexican than Spanish, but I kept my mouth shut about that.

- There were enough Native American students that I saw at least one in every class. All of them shot me the same look of both amusement and annoyance when I stared at them too long. I shouldn't have been surprised. Taos was built next to Taos Pueblo, a Native American settlement that was over a thousand years old. But I was still surprised. Knowing a thing and seeing it are two different experiences.

- It was hard to spot the cliques.

That last one spun me the most. In boarding school, there was a clear pecking order. In Taos, there were only the vestiges of one. I would have thought that a small town, with people who'd known each other from kindergarten on, would have a rigid caste system. But what appeared to have formed instead was a nebulous one. There were pretty girls who dressed to the nines, but they would stop and talk to frumpy girls who needed to find out what the assignment had been that day in class. There were super buff jocks, but they fraternized with gangly guys with acne. For that matter, the guys and the girls didn't keep a clear line of separation. Watching the cafeteria during lunch gave me the sense that I was looking at geological strata. There were today's alliances, but beneath those were yesterday's, and beneath those were elementary-school seating charts, parents who were best friends, and people who lived near each other. Old bonds didn't dissolve completely when new ones were formed.

By the end of the day, I'd somewhat shaken the feeling I was on a television show. Taos was its own place. Although it was unmistakably an American high school, it educated a very unique local population.

At least all of this provided some distraction while I searched for Corban. I saw him standing at the far end of the hall when I headed to third period, but he ducked out the door and was gone. At lunch, he was across the cafeteria, sitting with a girl who let her hair flop over her face as if to hide. He returned my gaze with one of annoyance and got up and left. After lunch, he was standing by the flagpole when I went outside, but gone in the time it took for me to blink. Whether or not I was a vampire, I was clearly a persona non grata, though I suspected he'd try to corner me again once I was alone. In the morning that terrified me, but by afternoon, I was desperate to talk to him again. We definitely had unfinished business to address.

I saw no sign of him when the last bell rang, though, and that made me wonder how the rest of the afternoon would go.

Would Aunt Cassie be home when I got there? Would Corban follow me to my bus or nab me on the walk home from the bus stop?

As I was packing my backpack with the sparse contents of my locker, Gina stepped up beside me.

"Hey," she said. "Amy and I are going to the grocery store. You want to come? I can drop you off at home after."

The grocery store? In boarding school, rides to the grocery store were a ticket out of the rarified atmosphere of campus and into the real world. It was where one could get junk food, magazines, cheap face wash, and fifty types of deodorant. Only seniors who'd turned eighteen could even drive to the grocery store, and people offered me rides when they needed something, like for me to agree to be their lab partner so that they could pass science.

Here, where it looked like most of the student body could drive, and where nobody lived on campus, I suspected Gina was not going to try to trade a ride for some favor. That meant she was being nice for no reason, or because she wanted to spend time with me.

It also meant I didn't have to face Aunt Cassie and her house for a while longer.

"Um, sure," I said, trying not to be awkward.

"Amy needs to get stuff to make tamales this weekend," she explained. "Her family didn't make them during Christmas because her brother was on deployment."

"Okay…"

She giggled. "I guess if you're not from around here, you don't care when people make tamales."

"Are they supposed to be a Christmas thing?"

"Yeah, according to Spanish tradition."

"Spanish, or Mexican?" I asked, the words out of my mouth before I could catch myself. If there was one thing I knew about not appearing racist, it was that asking questions along the lines of, "Don't you belong in this group not that one?" was a bad idea.

"Um, I dunno." She shrugged. "My ancestors chose to be Spanish rather than Native. They, like, intermarried with Spaniards and adopted Spanish traditions. Mexicans kinda came along later. And if you call someone Mexican it can kinda sound like you're saying they're not American. Like that they're here illegally or… whatever." Her second shrug was awkward.

But the light went on in my brain. "Got it," I said. She was Spanish in much the same way the Pennsylvania Dutch were Deutsch. "But… so Amy also does the Spanish traditions?" I hoped that I wasn't making an utter fool out of myself.

"Her family does tamales, yeah. There's a lot of mixing around here. Plenty of Anglos do tamales at Christmas too."

Amy slammed her locker shut a few slots down from me and turned to look at us, eyebrows slightly raised in query. Gina gave her a thumbs-up, and just like that, we headed out the door together.

WE PILED INTO Gina's white Ford compact sedan. Its seats were covered with plaid picnic blankets and the whole interior smelled like singed hair. I wondered if it was sheer sexism that kept me feeling calm, despite this. If Gina were Gino, I'd take the singed hair smell as a warning that he might try to set me on fire, but as it was, I climbed into the back seat while Amy clambered into the front, flipping her ponytail out of the way as she buckled her seat belt.

A chunky crystal hung from the rearview mirror and the floor was littered with fast food wrappers.

"So I thought you had studio today," Amy said as Gina buckled herself in to the driver's seat.

"No, tomorrow," she said. "Later today I've got a bunch of earrings to finish."

"Meaning you're spending how many hours of your apprenticeship doing basic wire wrap for free? You could learn more from running an Etsy store."

"Yeah, well, I'll spend all of Friday afternoon on the bench–"

"Oooh, one whole afternoon. Seriously, why can't you even call my uncle?" Amy paused, glanced over her shoulder at me, and explained. "She's working to become a jeweler."

The history of Taos being an artists' colony popped back into my mind. Art class hadn't been as intimidating as I feared it would be, but meeting someone my age who was learning jewelry making as anything other than a hobby was strange.

Gina looked back at me as well. "Amy does not approve of my apprenticeship to one of the top jewelers in Taos."

"He's not all that," said Amy. "And he's a terrible teacher. My family has, like, five jewelers in it who are better teachers. They just aren't as famous. And they're not Spanish."

This was clearly a sore spot because Gina whipped around. "My dad barely let me take an apprenticeship, okay? Stop blaming me for his issues."

"Okay, fine. I just think that you could work with one of my uncles and tell your dad you're hanging out at my house. Why let him control your life? He doesn't even know anything."

"I don't lie to my dad."

"But you should."

"You are an evil influence on me. Get thee behind me!" Gina made a clawing motion at Amy.

"Um… apprenticeship?" I hoped my butting in would diffuse the joking-but-not-really-joking debate in the front seat.

"Yeah, silversmithing. Eventually goldsmithing after I've done a year or so," said Gina.

"So in college?" I asked.

It was an innocent question, but I immediately realized my mistake when Gina gave a defensive shrug. "College isn't for everyone, you know?"

"Right," I said. "Sorry, I'm just clueless. I literally know nothing about jewelry making. I don't even know that much about jewelry buying, as any girl at my old school could tell you."

"Do you have any rich friends who want to be patrons of a jewelry line?" Gina asked, eyes hopeful.

"Um… I didn't really have any friends."

"Yeah, your old school sounds *great*," Amy muttered. She slapped the dashboard. "Come on. I need to get home."

"She has to go fetch well water and split firewood for her clan," said Gina.

"I can't be late for my vision quest, okay? Respect the Red Willow People!"

Much as I wanted in on the joke, I didn't want to keep replaying my "clueless newcomer" act. It was probably wearing thin on them. Instead I sat back while Gina pulled the car out of the parking lot, and then I watched the brown, earthen buildings of Taos scroll by as we drove to the grocery store.

Now when I say the buildings were brown and earthen, I mean all of them. Literally. Every building was either built from adobe or stuccoed to look like it was. The houses, strip malls, restaurants, fast-food joints, movie theater, everything. Vigas, the traditional roof beams that held the ceilings up, jutted out in neat rows across the fronts, each viga painted dark brown to preserve the wood. All of this, I knew, was a building style taken from Taos Pueblo, but I got the impression that nowadays it was part of Taos's brand. The city made most of its money from tourism and selling art, so even the back alleys were styled to make people feel they were somewhere exotic.

The cars slipping past were everything from brand-new Teslas to ancient, beat-up hatchbacks that had lost their badging, and even the grocery-store parking lot showed the full spectrum. Pristine BMWs were parked next to decrepit Honda Civics. It reminded me of Southampton a little bit, with its smattering of old-timer locals whose family trees predated the influx of big money. It was just that home had way more of the fancy cars and tended to crowd the locals out of all but the most inexpensive stores.

The grocery store facade was the same brown stucco with vigas jutting out in a row above the large front windows. The sign that proclaimed it part of a major chain stood out in odd juxtaposition, like it was a modern American convenience trying to insert itself into a third-world economy. I wondered exactly how badly I'd offend people if I repeated this observation aloud...

Gina and Amy led me through the front sliding doors, and it was as if we passed through a portal out of exotic Taos and into the generic American grocery store I'd seen countless times. This one was complete with a high ceiling and an errant mylar balloon resting against the metal trusses, an escapee from the floral department, no doubt. The air smelled like moisture and greenery and Pine Sol and the row of cash registers at the front were all beeping in time to the cashiers swiping bar codes across the sensors.

Amy and Gina had their heads together for a moment, then they turned to me. "So we can meet you at the cash registers in, like, fifteen minutes?"

I nodded. That gave me time to stock up on breakfast food other than stale Pop Tarts.

I fetched a plastic basket and struck out into the store, but the familiarity of the aisles faded upon closer inspection. The first one I went down had shelf upon shelf of religious candles, great big ones with saints printed on the outside of their glass containers. I wondered if they were a Catholic thing or a Spanish thing or what, and I wondered why they were in the grocery store next to the microwave popcorn.

"Are you religious?"

Corban's voice hit me like a rock between the shoulder blades and I tensed up accordingly. Then I made myself breathe and turn around. At least I wasn't alone here. There were plenty of people within earshot.

He leaned against the shelves opposite the candles and, much to my surprise, looked worse for wear. Gone was the ethereal, unshakeable guy who'd cornered me in the bathroom that morning. His hair now looked rumpled, like he'd run his fingers through it too many times, and his eyes looked tired, almost haunted.

For a moment he focused on my golden cross pendant and lifted an eyebrow. "Do you believe in God?" he asked.

It was none of his business. Unless… "Do vampires not?"

"No, I think they do, by and large. Crosses, if they've been sanctified, will burn them. Holy water, not so much. I mean, it depends on the source."

I wondered how I might find a sanctified cross to test on myself. Could I find a priest who would sanctify my necklace?

"Let me drive you home?" he asked. "I promise I won't hurt you, okay? We just really, *really-*" he leaned forward "-need to talk."

6

I was still scared of Corban, for obvious reasons, and my inner sexist did not want to get a ride home from a guy I didn't know, but my inner scientist needed to hear whatever he was willing to tell me about my condition. I hesitated, debating my options.

"If you want to write my social security number on your arm in permanent marker," he said, "I'll find you a marker."

"What?"

"It was in a Sandra Bullock movie."

"Okay..."

He held his palms up. "I'm just trying to be funny, and failing, obviously. I know you don't know me, is all I'm saying. I respect that you'd have reservations, so whatever I can do to set you at ease, let me know."

"You could still cut my arm off, or slash it up, or burn my body–"

"Yeah, you must be a fun blind date, you know that? How 'bout you call your aunt. She knows who I am, and despite appearances, she's a good judge of character."

My aunt… I winced and got out my phone. She would be expecting me to come home on the bus and I hadn't let her know that I'd gotten a ride with Gina. I dialed her number.

"Liana," she answered her phone.

"Hi, sorry. I'm just letting you know that I got a ride with a friend and will be home a little late. I'm at the grocery store."

She was silent for so long that I wondered if the connection had dropped.

Corban stayed put, arms folded across his muscular chest.

"Look," said Aunt Cassie, "thank you for thinking of me, but let's get one thing straight. I never wanted to be a parent, and I'd be terrible at it if I tried."

"O-okay…"

"So I'm not going to try. You're old enough to figure stuff out for yourself and rich enough that you can buy your way out of most scrapes. I wish you the best of luck. No need to update me on the details."

"Oh…"

"No offense, okay? I love you. You're the only family I have left. I get to be the irresponsible one, though. You can't take that title from me. I don't care if you're the teenager, I claim seniority in being irresponsible. Understand?"

"Yeah, I think so."

"Good."

"Do you know Corban… um… Corban–"

"Alexander," he supplied.

"Right. You know Corban Alexander?" I asked.

"Only by reputation. Every girl in town has a massive crush on him, it seems. He's a Boy Scout, so if you're thinking you're going to win his heart, you probably won't. If you did, it'd probably be boring. He'll have you home by eight o'clock and shake your hand good night."

She said these things like they were negatives, but they put me at ease. "He's going to give me a ride home."

"He's probably just being friendly. Don't say I didn't warn you."

"I'll be fine with… all that. Thanks."

We hung up and I turned to face him again. "I'll ride home with you, but I need to find Gina and tell her, and I need to get some breakfast cereal and stuff."

Amy came jogging up right then, though, and stepped right in front of Corban as if he wasn't even there. "Hey, so can you handle spice, or are you too New York for that?"

"Um… probably too New York?" I ventured.

"Got it." She turned to leave.

"Hey, I'm going to get a ride home with Corban, if that's okay?" *Please don't press me for details*, I thought.

She glanced up at Corban and nearly jumped out of her skin. "Ohmigosh, I did not see you there." She laughed. "Yeah, cool. Okay."

Gina appeared at the far end of the aisle and Amy headed back to meet her.

Corban did not seem the least bit fazed by this. "Good call on the spice," he said. "You're clearly getting your bearings here."

"I don't even know why she was asking."

"Well, it's probably related to you eating food with her at some point. Like tamales this weekend."

That had sounded like a family affair, but perhaps Amy would give me some of the tamales they made? That would be sweet of her, and did make the conversation make a lot more sense.

"You get what you need," said Corban, "and then let's go."

I hitched my plastic basket a little higher up on my forearm and headed down the aisle towards breakfast foods. Corban followed me, close enough so that it was clear we were together and far enough apart that I didn't feel crowded.

I grabbed a box of muesli and tossed that in my basket, then slowed and stopped in front of the Pop Tarts. The ones I'd had this morning had been disgusting, but what if Aunt Cassie insisted I keep on eating them? Maybe if I got a better flavor, I'd hate those less? The problem was, none of the flavors looked appetizing and several made my stomach lurch.

Corban looked on, curious.

I finally grabbed a box of brown sugar and cinnamon and tossed it in my basket.

Corban tagged along behind me as I stopped to get milk, then went to the front registers to pay. I caught a glimpse of Gina and Amy pushing a cart full of shopping bags out the doors, but they didn't glance back, so they didn't see me.

The checker who scanned my items was a very bored-looking older woman who didn't so much as glance at Corban. I paid with my prepaid credit card and gathered my one bag, feeling awkward all of a sudden, which was better than feeling terrified. I was about to be alone with Corban, again, and even though he promised not to hurt me, he hadn't made the best first impression on that score.

He brushed past me and out the front doors, so I followed him into the frigid air of the parking lot, where he led me to a bright, metallic turquoise Toyota RAV-4. I couldn't help but stare at it, since it screamed its existence so forcefully with that color.

The cars people drove in the Hamptons or at the Hawke Academy were always white, black, gray, or if the person was feeling adventurous, champagne. Any car worth having was a feat of precision engineering that could cruise at seventy miles an hour with an engine so silent that one could whisper to the people in the back seat. It was uncouth for someone to call attention to their car with a bright color, or if one insisted on being uncouth, the agreed-upon loud color was red. Perhaps yellow. Never bright blue, and definitely not metallic bright blue.

Corban unlocked and opened the back, then turned to me. "What? You don't like my car?"

"Um… do you really care what I think?" I asked.

"Yeah, I kind of do." He took my grocery bag, put it in his car, then slammed the back hatch shut and gestured for me to get into the passenger seat.

He cared what vampires thought about his car?

The interior was spotless. There were no wrappers, cans, discarded straws, not even lint on the floor. It looked as if it had just been vacuumed. There were also vanilla-scented air fresheners clipped to the air vents.

I began to wonder if Corban was gay. I didn't like to stereotype, but…

"So it's not a Mercedes," he said, defensively, as he climbed into the driver's seat. "I know you're used to better."

"Oh, no, I don't care about that," I said. "And I like the blue. It stands out."

"Not around here it doesn't." He pointed through the windshield at another bright blue car, then another, then another. "You're in the land of turquoise jewelry and deep blue skies. This car is New Mexico's idea of understated."

He started the engine, shifted into gear, and soon we were back on the main road. One thing about Taos was that it was hard to get lost. It had one road that went through the entire town in a long, arcing curve. Even my aunt's subdivision was on this road, if one drove to the far end of town and beyond.

Corban, however, drove to the plaza, another part of town I knew about from the Wikipedia page. Apparently all the notable towns in northern New Mexico had plazas, which were central squares surrounded by hotels, restaurants, boutiques, and art galleries. Before turning off the main road, though, he said, "There's a cafe we can go to, if that's all right?"

A cafe was a good, public space. The milk that I'd just stashed in his car would probably be okay, given it was winter and the outside temperature was cold enough to make people's breath mist. "Okay," I agreed.

He drove down some narrow little streets and parked in a lot near a cluster of buildings that proved to be a shopping village. We got out and he led me towards it. These structures all looked relatively new, and the place boasted a kitchen shop, a bookstore, and several clothing boutiques, that I could see. The architecture here was a little different; these had peaked metal roofs and white-painted wood window frames and doors. The walls were the same stucco as the rest of the city.

"Do you like cats?" Corban asked as he held open a door for me. "Coffee Cats," read the neon hued sign in the window.

I had no opinion on cats, per se, and decided to take Corban's question as rhetorical. After all, there were no actual cats that I could see or smell inside the cafe. It was a small space with tables along one wall and a wooden floor that my boots thunked against hollowly.

The menu, posted above the ordering counter, was entirely cat-themed. On it were items like a "fluffy cat" (cappuccino) and a "cat's meow" (latte.) Regular coffee was called a "house cat". I didn't want to drink caffeine this late in the day because I had enough trouble sleeping as it was, so I ordered a "decaf lily cat" from the woman behind the counter. This was a vanilla latte, apparently. Before I could get my wallet out, Corban leaned past me with a five dollar bill pinched between his index and middle fingers. The woman plucked it from him and rang me up, handing him back change that he tossed into the tip jar.

I'd never had a guy buy me coffee before, and it didn't seem to square with why we were meeting here, but I figured I shouldn't be awkward about it so I just thanked him and tucked my wallet away.

It also made me nervous that he got nothing for himself, but again, I didn't say anything and I tried very hard not to imagine all the ways I could dump coffee on myself while he just looked on. Being the only one with a drink was like having an audience.

My latte was ready in seconds, and I followed Corban into the seating area, past a couple who were having a very tense conversation. At the sight of Corban, both of them sat back and took deep breaths, visibly willing themselves to calm down.

The seating area turned out to be L-shaped, but still small. We went around the corner to the table farthest from the front door.

"This okay?" Corban asked, pulling out a chair.

I nodded and sat down in the other chair, hoping that didn't seem too standoffish. Just because we could get through a few minutes of normal conversation did not mean that this situation was at all normal. There was no point in me pretending like we were on a flirty date. He didn't seem to mind as he sat himself down and put his forearms on the table between us, his hands folded. His nails were neat and even; he clearly didn't ever chew on them like I did mine. His overall demeanor was relaxed, casual. Like this morning, his bearing evoked the feeling that we were old friends rather than barely acquainted strangers. Not even his slightly disheveled appearance changed that.

I set my latte down carefully, proud that it didn't slosh over the brim.

"So," he said, "you say the sun burns you at sunrise?" He spoke so quietly that if anyone across the room had coughed, they would have drowned him out.

I nodded.

"How many sunrises have you seen?"

"I dunno. Seven? Eight?"

His eyes widened. "Really?"

"Look, have you decided about the whole... killing-me thing?" I asked. "I mean, I know you promised not to right now, but is that your for-sure position?"

"I won't hurt you in any way while you're like this," he said.

Like what? I wondered. I took a sip of my latte and hoped he'd fill the silence with an explanation.

He pressed his fingertips to the table, an odd kind of fidget that made me wonder if he played guitar. "As best as I can tell," he said, "you're not fully turned."

I dabbed the foam from my upper lip with my napkin and again waited for him to say more.

"My guess is that you've got all the prerequisites to be a vampire, but you haven't finished the transition, and you reset the process every morning at sunrise."

"So I'm in, like, vampire remission?" I asked.

"More like you're undergoing radiation treatment which is keeping you alive for now. See, the way things typically work is that a vamp drinks from you, you drink from them, and you transition. I had to dig to find out that there are some accounts of people turned right before sunrise who lived through that day without turning. The sunshine somehow knocks the vampirism back, and the process can't resume until sundown, or if you stayed indoors too long, I guess."

I folded my now-shaking hands in my lap. "So, any night I could just turn the whole way?"

"I'm really wondering why you haven't already. Are you a really... conservative person? I don't mean politically. I mean, do you tend to go to bed early and not get yourself into trouble?"

"I got bitten by a vampire," I said.

"Was that out of character for you?"

I shrugged. Didn't it reveal my character? "I thought I was a boring nerd before this all happened. I have nerd-like habits, but only when I don't have an option to be more... adventurous."

He looked me straight in the eye.

I drew myself inward.

His gaze didn't let up. "Have you ever used your super speed?" he asked.

"Huh?"

"Like, running really fast?" he asked.

I remembered how Evan could fly across the room in the blink of an eye. "No. I've never done that."

"Ever gone into mist form?"

"What form?"

"You know, vampires can dissolve into mist–and do not question me about the physics or the biology or anything like that." He spread his hands. "I don't know how it works. It just does. It's how vamps get out of locked rooms and chests and stuff like that."

"I thought it was bats," I said. "Don't we turn into bats?"

"No, blame Hollywood for that one, I think. It's mist, not bats. I take it the answer is no?"

"Pretty sure I haven't."

"Super strength?"

I shook my head.

"Fed on any humans?"

"No…"

"Then suffice it to say, you turn down all kinds of opportunities to be more adventurous. You're holding off vampirism by pure force of will." His gaze conveyed sincere respect.

Which I did not deserve. "Being a boring person," I said, "doesn't require strength."

"Yeah, it does, actually."

I looked down at my folded hands and shook my head. "When a cute guy showed interest in me," I said. "I got bitten and fed on and went along with it. The person I thought I was? The prude who would have sent the guy away and focused on studying instead? That turned out to be a lie. I'm not strong."

He lifted one eyebrow. "Riiight, do you think a weak person would be able to say what you just said to a virtual stranger like me?"

"So I'm socially awkward too." I shrugged.

"Liana, listen, I don't know you very well, but I do know vampirism. People don't conquer it, ever. Not day after day. It's never happened before in history."

"How would you know?" I asked.

"My order keeps records of this kind of stuff."

"Your… order?"

"My organization. The vampire hunters."

I let that sink in. "Is your whole family in the order?"

"All of my relatives I know of are in it."

"So your parents are?"

He pressed his fingertips to the tabletop again. "I lost my parents a while ago, and I really don't want to talk about it."

"Sure."

"Sorry. It's just… yeah. Personal." His gaze strayed to the wall a moment, then came back to me.

"Right." I nodded. "Sorry to pry."

"Well, you didn't, actually. Anyway, let's talk about you being the first of your kind in history?"

I sipped more latte, then pointed out, "You didn't find me until I moved to your town. There could be others like me that you don't know about, right?"

"Fine. Sure."

"Unless your order has really detailed records and there are a lot of you or you have some way to track all vampires or–"

He held up a hand. "I totally understand your curiosity, but I can't answer many questions about myself or my order. You're a human now, but probably not for long. You're also very smart, so I can't afford to tell you things that your brain will hang onto once your body loses its soul. You're going to be one dangerous vamp as it is."

I considered this. If it was just an excuse to stonewall me, it was a cleverly constructed one that played on my vanity. There was one question I needed the answer to all the same. "Will anyone else in your order try to kill me? Is your decision to let me live, like, binding on everyone?"

"Let me worry about stuff like that. You live your life."

"And ignore the potential death strike that could–"

"No, don't worry about that. As long as you're human and you're here in Taos, you're safe. As for staying human, I'm going to lay out some rules, all right?"

I bit my lip. I was done with letting pretty boys dictate my life to me, but I figured I'd listen to what these rules were before I argued further.

7

Corban ran his fingers through his hair, rumpling it still more so that he looked like a mad scientist. An oddly young and hot mad scientist.

I took another sip of latte to break that train of thought.

"First off, don't stay out past sundown," he said.

"Would a UV lamp keep the vampirism out of my system?"

He shook his head.

"A full spectrum–"

"It has to be sunlight," he said. "Trust me, every other possible option has been tried. Vamps can handle UV lamps, full spectrum lamps, every approximation for sunlight that is technologically possible. Only the real deal affects them."

I bit my lip and considered that. "So if I moved really far south–"

"Stay in Taos for now."

"But I could get more hours of sunlight if I went south."

He nodded. "True, and that's a fair point. Let me see if I can make moving safe for you, but right now, you really need to stay in Taos."

"Why?"

"Because this is my area and I can make sure no one hurts you while you're here."

"Your area?"

"Yeah." He shrugged as if this was no big deal.

"There aren't any adults overseeing this area? Just you?"

He pursed his lips, mulling over his answer, I could tell. Finally he said, "Yeah, it's just me. The order has people of all ages and we all have responsibilities. That's how it works."

"Okay, so if I set one foot outside Taos city, I'm dead? Or does this cover the county?"

"Just stick around the city, okay?"

"Can I go visit the pueblo? Are shopping trips to Santa Fe out of the question? What about Taos Ski Valley?"

He put his hands over his face, which I suspected was to cover him rolling his eyes.

Which he had no business doing. My questions were valid.

"Um…" he said, "the ski valley is fine, the pueblo is fine. I'll give you my cell phone number and you text me if you're going anywhere else, all right?"

"No," I said. "Not all right. I barely know you and for all I know you're just a nutcase living some delusion that you're a vampire hunter."

"Okay, fine. How about this? I will give you my phone number and ask that you please text me. You're right that I don't control you. It's up to you whether or not you trust me."

He wasn't doing anything to double down or make demands, which made me think that this really wasn't about control for him. That didn't sway me completely, but it was enough for me to nod so we could move on to the next topic.

"So, my number," he said. "If you look through the sent texts on your phone, you'll see one I sent to myself, so that I'd have your number."

"Oh."

"If you want to move somewhere with longer days, let me know."

"I want to move somewhere with longer days," I said.

This time he didn't hide his eye roll, but it wasn't one of disgust. He was scrambling, trying to stay on top of a situation that was too big for him. "If you leave the state, I need to talk to a higher-up who I have… issues with. If you leave the country, I have to deal with an even higher higher-up who hates everything vampire with a passion. He will kill you. Or he'll try. If you want to fight him, I can't help you, okay? Even if I sympathize with you, the hierarchy is everything in my order. I have to stand aside."

I sipped more latte. "Fine," I said. "But I still want to move, okay? Just, file that away as a fact about me."

"Noted. Okay, the next rules are obvious: don't use any vampire powers. I'm pretty sure that if you do, you'll turn fully vampire and die in the next sunrise."

"Are those the ones you listed?" I asked. "Super speed, mist form, super strength, and feeding off people?"

"Yeah, well, the feeding isn't a power, but don't do it either."

"And only human blood works to feed a vampire?" I remembered how Evan had said he'd tried animal blood.

"Human blood straight from a human. All the television shows and stuff where vamps drink from animals or blood banks are a lie. And a nightmare for my order. Do you have any idea how many more cases of vampirism there have been ever since Hollywood made it sexy? I mean… for centuries vampires were these fearsome bogeymen and we almost had them hunted to extinction, but then modern culture decides maybe vampires are misunderstood and…" He made a gesture like an explosion on the tabletop, spreading the fingers of both hands.

Then he caught himself. "Sorry. I don't mean to rant."

I shrugged.

He sat back, shut his eyes a moment, then leaned forward to put his elbows on the table again. "Vampires suck life directly from individual humans. That's how it works. There is literally no other way to keep a vampire alive. But don't experiment with drinking any kind of blood."

"Aw, way to ruin my plans for Friday night," I said. Now it was my turn to roll my eyes.

He laughed. "Yeah, rein it in. If you need to do something wild, paint your toenails a fluorescent color or something."

When I didn't laugh, his face fell.

"So, yeah…" he said. "The other thing I need you to do, you won't like."

"What is it?"

"Let me into your bedroom."

"Why?"

"I want to do a spell to separate your room from your aunt's house."

"So... if I turn, I can't get into the rest of the house?" I asked. "The room will be my home and the rest of the house Cassie's?"

"Right."

"Okay, yes," I said. "Definitely. Let's do that."

"I... keep forgetting who I'm talking to." He clearly thought I was the weirdest vampire he'd ever met.

"So my aunt will be protected if she's in her part of the house?" I asked.

"She should be."

"Wait... What do you mean, should?"

"The protection spell on homes isn't fully understood. It's a pretty good safeguard, but every now and then there's a house it doesn't work on." He shrugged.

"It's a spell? There's a spell on everyone's house?"

"There's a good chance it's actually a group of spells that have been handed down and altered over centuries. They activate automatically, when they activate. Coverage is a little patchy. Sometimes only part of a house is covered, some houses are, like, bulletproof. I only know the spell to separate one house into two homes. Nobody's cracked any of the original threshold spells."

"How does someone activate a spell they don't even know exists?" I asked. "Is it, like, if you have your name on a deed, that activates it?"

"That does not activate a protection spell. Believe me, that is the holy grail of protection spells, but nobody's ever made it work. Like I said, we really don't know what activates them. Taking one's shoes off at the door is a good practice."

"Bathing inside the house?"

"A likely factor, yeah."

"Having intimate relations?"

"Yeah… about that… only if it's with someone you're married to. I'm not saying that to be judgmental, it's just baked into the relevant spells. People who have affairs sometimes negate the protections on their houses."

"Sometimes?" I asked.

"Right. Not always. And we can't figure out what causes that discrepancy. And there are always cases where random places that are not homes and probably never have been are protected."

"Can you tell me where any of those are here in town?" I asked.

He shook his head. "You only find out if you're running from a vamp and they stop. Even places that worked a month ago might not work now. Like I said–"

"You can't figure out how the protection spells work," I interrupted. "You've figured out factors but not rules."

"Yes." He nodded.

"So, maybe stuff like cutting your toenails in a place activates the spell?"

"Um…" He paused.

"I was joking," I said.

"I actually want to try to drive a vamp into a nail salon now," he said. "I wonder if you're onto something."

It wasn't clear to me if he was being serious. He wasn't looking at me, expecting a laugh like he had with his previous jokes.

"Anyway," he said, shaking himself, "yeah, let me section off your room as a separate dwelling to up the odds that your aunt will be safe. And other than that, keep doing what you're doing."

I couldn't really argue with any of his rules, because they weren't really his rules. He was advising me on the rules of the universe and this mysterious order of his, not pushing me around. "Okay," I said.

"All right. You ready to go?"

I drained the rest of my latte, which had cooled a lot by now. That was one thing about being at such a high elevation, water boiled at a lower temperature. After I patted the last of the foam off my upper lip, we got up to go.

THIS WAS THE second time I was riding from Taos to my aunt's house, and the first time I was doing it in daylight. I'd done it the other way this morning, obviously, but it was nevertheless stunning once more.

Taos Valley had the enormous Taos Gorge running through it, and I think that's a misnomer. Or maybe I just don't know dramatic land features. This thing was a full-on *canyon*, and that canyon was between the town of Taos and the far-flung subdivision where my aunt lived.

Apparently her address still had a Taos zip code and such, but I didn't really know how all of that stuff worked. All I knew was that Corban drove out of the town I'd attended high school in and into the open desert. Ahead was the gorge/canyon. There was a bridge across, and I don't know bridge design very well, but this bridge was the kind that was entirely supported from underneath, rather than being a suspension bridge that had cables and things jutting up.

This meant that to drive across this bridge meant looking at solid ground one moment and a chasm the next. I craned my neck to see as far down the canyon as I could, and could not see the bottom. It was shrouded in shadow between sheer cliffs and the very sight of it gave me the sensation I was falling.

"Yeah," muttered Corban. "You're not strong at all."

"Huh?"

"You're staring down into the gorge."

I turned to face him. "You're afraid of heights?"

"Um, no. I'm afraid of falling from great heights, though. It's called being a normal person."

I considered that. "Well," I said, "if I jumped I could survive by turning to mist. So I wouldn't die immediately, and what I'm hearing you say is you wouldn't jump after me…"

"I'm not sure whether to be impressed with your logic or weirded out by it."

"Yeah, you wouldn't be much fun on a blind date either," I quipped. Then my heart began to pound as I realized what I'd said. I'd used the word "date"–and it didn't matter that he'd used it first. It felt much more presumptuous coming out of my mouth.

But he laughed, hard. "Touché," he said, and continued to chuckle as we drove past the bridge and to the turn into my aunt's subdivision. It was an odd subdivision, with lots roughly the size of what might be normal for nice houses in the Hamptons, but without any greenery or visual interest of any kind, really. They were just big brown lots of dirt, scrub, the occasional large boulder, and the houses, which all had the same bizarre architecture as my aunt's. Big windows for solar heat, oddly blobular and rounded walls made of tires, and organic-looking outcroppings that jutted from the main, rectangular-ish shapes.

I slumped down in my seat.

He finally stopped laughing and glanced at me. "What?" he asked. "That was a good one."

"I didn't mean to imply that this was… you know… never mind." I was making this so much worse.

But Corban didn't give me an annoyed look or roll his eyes or anything like that. He looked over at me, and actually looked. His eyes focused on mine before he turned back to the road. "You think you're not strong because you've got self-confidence issues," he said.

Was that true?

"About guys, at least," he said.

Yeah, I was way more embarrassed now than I was five minutes ago. Was he about to give me some kind of dad lecture on self-confidence?

He said nothing, though, just let that statement hang in the air.

I expected that to increase the tension between us, drawing it tighter and tighter until I wanted to die to escape, but it didn't. The words didn't linger and dig in. They dissipated as if they were some innocuous statement about the weather.

Since he'd uttered those last words, it was my turn to talk, and I felt like I had enough time to think before I said, "Well, yeah. That's how I ended up like this, you could say. You know, bitten."

"Yeah, that's pretty common. Not just for girls, for guys too. They're being hit on by this gorgeous person who seems so far out of their league and they let that person take liberties. I hesitate to call that weakness."

"It's a weakness," I said, unsure of what greater point I was driving at. Perhaps I was splitting hairs.

"True… but it's a regular human weakness. I mean, who would you be without it? Some totally arrogant person incapable of feeling flattered? Incapable of getting swept away by romance? What kind of life is that?"

I considered that, then said, "I think I needed better judgment. I should have trusted the feeling that he was out of my league."

"That makes me sad. I'll be honest. Turning away from something that makes you happy because you feel like you don't deserve it?"

"No, I'm not saying that," I protested. "I mean, forget vampires. It's just a safety issue. You gotta know that the person you're with doesn't have some ulterior motive. Most users are regular old humans and they're still dangerous."

"Well, true," he said. "But the girl I met today is very practical about that kind of stuff, and shouldn't be beating up on herself for letting herself believe the fairy tale was possible."

"It wasn't a fairy tale," I said. "I hated myself the whole time."

He looked at me again. "Did he force you?"

"Sometimes. Kind of. I mean…"

"Okay, that's just abuse. Do not beat up on yourself for being a victim of abuse."

"I'm beating up on myself for having this–this *condition* that I assume is incurable. That'll probably cut my life short."

"Well, let me see what else I can find out, okay?"

I wasn't sure whether to say, "Okay," or nod, or what. What exactly was he going to do to "find out" anything? He said his order had never heard of anyone like me. Did this mean he had other resources? That he wouldn't share with me?

As much as I felt that I had a right to information about my condition, I did understand why he couldn't give it to me. The more I knew about vampirism, the more I'd know about ways to kill vampires, which put him in danger. This wasn't about me having to trust him. It was about understanding why he couldn't trust me, and it was a fair reason.

"Okay," I said. Then, "Thank you. The whole not-killing-me-outright thing? I appreciate that."

"Don't mention it." His smile was wry.

I wondered if my thinking that I was a justifiable murder target for him was also me having self-confidence issues. That I would have to think about.

He pulled up to Aunt Cassie's house and turned off the car. "Okay if I come in?" he asked.

Aunt Cassie had no garage, so it was quite obvious that she wasn't home. Having Corban come in felt more than a little irresponsible.

Then again, what did I really think was going to happen? If he wanted to hurt me, he'd had enough opportunities.

I opened my mouth to say yes, then paused. "I'm not inviting you." I said. "But I'll leave the door open."

8

I was halfway to the back/front/whatever-it-was door of the house when Corban got out of his car. "I'm not a vampire," he called after me.

I nodded, opened the door, and stepped through, leaving it open behind me. The house might still have been strange and made of refuse, but in this moment, it felt like a home because it felt like shelter. The scent of the moist soil of the downstairs planter and the babble of the waterfall comforted me.

Corban was still out by the car, and he gave me a pointed look before going around to the back and retrieving my bag of groceries.

Yeah, that was embarrassing. I wasn't sure what to say as he walked up to stand on the other side of the threshold, his body silhouetted because of the dimness in the kitchen.

I stayed where I was in the middle of the kitchen, doing my best to conceal my surprise that he really did seem to have an issue with coming in. This had been a real long shot on my part.

The waterfall provided some nice white noise that meant I didn't have to listen to my heart pound.

He looked around, then reached forward and held out the bag of groceries. A few blinks later, and he'd stepped through the door. "I'm not a vampire," he repeated. "But you're smart to be cautious."

"Me inviting a vampire in… would it work if it isn't my house?" I asked. I took the bag from him and put the milk in the fridge and the Pop Tarts and cereal in the pantry.

"Depends," he said. "Again, it goes to the theory that there are a few different spells that protect the home." He cast his gaze around at the crazy patterns of glass bottles in the walls and the plywood cabinetry, and then asked, "Where's your room?"

I pointed and let him go first, only he refused. He turned and gestured for me to precede him.

"You afraid I left bras draped over the furniture?" I asked.

"I don't want to intrude."

"Do I need to be in my room at the same time as you when you do whatever you do?" If I didn't have to be near him while he did the spell, I was staying away. He'd been fine so far, but I wasn't following him into a more enclosed space. It just didn't seem smart.

"No… you don't need to be in your room. I figured you'd want to be so you can see what I'm doing."

"Leave the door open," I said.

He looked at me with respect, but I didn't care. This whole situation was strange, so there was no point wasting energy pretending to be cool with it.

"Okay, yeah, I can do that." He opened the door to reveal my room, which I hadn't gotten much of a look at in the daylight. It also had the glass bottles in a great big swirl on the domed ceiling, but the floor was like cobblestone, but with glass pebbles. It actually felt kind of good to walk on–like a foot massage–but it looked weird.

A rug which looked like a bath mat bought at a garage sale was at the foot of the bed, and there was a full-length mirror on the far wall with a frame made out of the same river rock and concrete that was behind the waterfall.

There was a chair, out of my line of sight, that was a strange wicker contraption that was roughly cylindrical with an oval cutout and an ill-fitting cushion that was an odd light turquoise. I had noted that this morning.

Though it did go nicely with the floral comforter on the bed. Randomly, that was Laura Ashley, because my aunt couldn't seem to stay consistent in breaking every rule of normalcy and design. That comforter was exactly like what girls in the Hawke Academy used.

Corban looked everything over with a clinical eye. "So…" he said, "I'm going to kneel and cast a spell here."

"Okay." That was probably one of the least random things that had ever happened in this house.

With another glance back at me, he got down on his knees and I winced in sympathy. The glass pebble floor did not look like it would feel good jammed into the soft tissue under the kneecap, but aside from a slight tensing of the shoulders, Corban endured it.

Whatever he said was quiet, barely a whisper, so I couldn't pick out the words. It was also short, because a moment later he was done and getting back to his feet.

"So," said Aunt Cassie right behind me.

I spun around, my heart thundering like it was going to burst out of my chest.

She wore a triumphant grin and the same bathrobe and slippers she'd been clad in that morning. "The Mormons already dedicated this house," she said. "Those kids wouldn't stop knocking and given how far they had to travel to see me, I didn't want to turn them away with nothing."

"What?" I asked. "What are you talking about?"

"The missionaries. You know, the Mormons send those little teenage boys around knocking on doors."

"You had them do what?" I was still confused.

"Dedicate the house. They offered. Said it would protect me from evil, and who can't use some extra protection from evil, right?"

Corban by now had regained his feet and stepped stiffly over to stand next to me.

"He's not a Mormon," I said, jabbing a thumb in his direction. Then I paused. "Are you? I mean, I assume–"

"Not exactly," he said.

"It would explain your reputation," said Cassie. "Pretty boy like you never having a girlfriend."

"Cassie…" I said.

"I'm probably too uptight for even the Latter-day Saints." Corban gave a good-natured shrug.

"And you know that about yourself, bravo." Cassie clearly approved.

"Where is your car?" I asked. My brain was still playing catch up.

"I parked it outside."

"Wait, you just came back?"

"Uh-huh. Why?" She put one hand on her hip and stood with her body at a cocky angle. "You want to impose a dress code? In Taos? Good luck with that."

"Um… yeah. No," I said. "I didn't hear the door open." But now that I thought about it, that wasn't all that shocking. There was, after all, a *waterfall* running through the kitchen at all times.

"I was over at Lydia's. She's bringing dinner over in an hour. Corban can stay. Well, any of your friends or enemies or pets or whatever can stay. You don't need my permission. I would rather you not put me in the position of having to grant it."

"So if I bring an elephant in here–"

"There will be an actual elephant in the room that we won't talk about. Or I won't, at least." She strolled over to the stairs and started on down.

I turned back to Corban. "Do you know who Lydia is?" I asked under my breath.

He leaned in so that he could speak softly right in my ear, his breath tickling the tiny hairs on my skin. "Lydia Garcia, single mom of three who your aunt pays as a private chef."

"Oh."

He pulled back so he could shout, "It was nice to see you, Cassie!" down the stairs.

"Liana, see if you can get him to even shake your hand," she called back.

I put my hands in my pockets and hoped he wouldn't ask.

But he didn't bat an eye. "You need anything else?"

I still had more questions for him, but my brain was tired and there was always tomorrow. "No, thanks," I said. "I hope what you did works."

"You need to make sure your aunt never invites you into the rest of the house."

"Okay…" I wondered if it had to be a formal invitation, or if her shouting, "Liana, get in here!" would suffice. I also wondered if there was a way for me to talk her into clipping her toenails in the kitchen, right outside my door. That didn't seem as hard as something like that ought to be.

"I'll see you around, okay?" said Corban.

I nodded. "See you."

He exited the house and shut the door behind him. I listened, and realized I couldn't hear his engine starting or anything like that. That waterfall drowned out a lot. If I ever was in a position of needing to know whether marauders were congregating outside the house, I'd need to find out how to turn the pump off.

"Well," said Cassie, startling me again. She was back at the top of the stairs. "What did you do to him? I've never seen him like that."

"I didn't do anything. He drove me home from the grocery store and…" I tried to think of an excuse to cover for what he was doing in my room.

She waited, hand on her hip.

I was fast hitting my limit of weirdness for the day, though. "How 'bout I just say that he was putting up a ward against… vampires? Okay?"

She blinked.

And I felt incredibly stupid. "I mean…"

"Vampires?"

"Just, wait. He was…"

"Is that why you look so different from your family Christmas card picture?"

I bit my lip.

"It's crazy for me to say you might be a vampire, right?" pressed Cassie.

"Yes."

"Okay."

"But, just to be safe, don't invite me into the house, ever. If I ever seem stuck in my room, get away."

"All right."

"And if you want me to leave–"

"No, I do not. This is your home, okay? You don't have to worry about finding food and shelter, and there's internet so you can look up doctors or whatever if you actually do think there are vampires out to get you. I'm sorry I can't provide any kind of role model or much in the way of emotional support, but what shreds of sanity I have left, you're welcome to. Just don't expect me to be there in a crisis. I wish I was reliable like that, but I kind of don't, really."

"Okay… Thank you."

"I will say this. I expected you to be a lot more boring."

"Normally I am."

"This last, like, fifteen minutes? Truly, truly strange." She said it like a sincere compliment.

"Sorry."

"Don't be sorry. But do take care of yourself." She turned and headed back down the stairs.

"Can I drink coffee?" I called after her.

"What, right now?" She paused and turned.

"No, tomorrow morning."

"If you're willing to get us a bigger coffeemaker. Or if you're willing to do two pots."

"Yeah, I can do that."

"Then yeah. I just need my big bowl of coffee in the morning. It's my ritual. Don't mess with it."

That was far more reasonable of a response than I'd expected. Which said more about my expectations than her reasonableness.

"Do I have to eat Pop Tarts?" I asked.

"Well, I hate them but I also hate waste."

"If I make the Pop Tarts disappear, can we call it good?"

She nodded. "As long as I don't see them in the trash or anything like that."

"Okay," I said.

"Okay. Good talk. I feel almost like a grown-up, so let's not make a habit of this." She headed on down the stairs.

I watched her go, then wished fervently that I had more than a measly two hours of homework.

THE NEXT MORNING, I woke up to find my hand resting on my journal, which was open to a page about Corban. I almost pushed it away onto the floor.

But sunrise was coming and I had to prepare, so I threw off my covers just as the sun peeked above the horizon. The now-familiar feeling of being drenched in molten metal began at once.

Today I didn't just allow the pain to happen. I embraced it, grateful for the cleansing feeling. If everywhere that hurt was everywhere I'd been afflicted with vampirism, I was eager to have it burned away.

Once the pain subsided, I sat up and looked in the mirror. It was difficult to feel pure happiness about having a reflection, though, because of what the reflection showed. My face was perfectly symmetrical with high cheekbones and flawless skin. Even my hair looked decent after a night of sleeping on it. I wasn't critical of how I looked the way an actual pretty girl would be. The face in the mirror wasn't mine.

My gaze fell on my notebook again. I flipped it shut and got up to put it in my backpack, only to sit back down on my bed, drop the journal, and put my head in my hands. I didn't want to dwell on feeling ashamed of how far into strangeness my conversations with Corban had gone the day before. When I examined my behavior, I didn't see anything specific to be ashamed of. He'd been the source of the weirdness, following me around, even into the girls' bathroom, and calling me a vampire.

Besides, what he'd said about vampires did, truly, conform to my experiences.

But it was still weird and I wanted, so badly, to have my boring and normal life back. The shame even overlaid the ever-present grief of losing my father. Why couldn't I have the time and space to process that?

The journal had fallen with its pages splayed open to the page on Corban, hardly surprising since that's where it had been open all night. I read it over with as critical an eye as I could manage. It wasn't the rambling of a lovesick schoolgirl, I didn't think. It was rational and contained observations and information, which was what I always recorded in my journal. Still, I didn't want my future self or my children or whoever might read my journal to read about me taking vampires seriously.

I reached down and, with a little bit of struggle, managed to rip the page out cleanly. My wallet was in my backpack, which was on the chair, so I stashed the page there, focusing carefully on the feeling of folding the paper and putting it away from me.

Now, maybe I could face this day.

THE FIRST THING I saw when I stepped off the bus at school was two guys shoving each other, with a loose ring of students around them to watch the action.

Gina was approaching from off to my left, moving apart from the crowd, her posture a display of disbelief and confusion.

I headed for her.

She spotted me when I was about five yards away and came towards me.

"Is this normal?" I asked.

Shouts of the teachers were breaking up the crowd now, and students were peeling off and dashing for the school entrance, eager not to be seen as making the situation worse.

"It's normal for Sean and Lance to hate each other," she replied. "I've never seen them fight." She seemed shaken up, as if she'd never seen anyone fight before.

Maybe they cracked down on that sort of thing more in public high schools. In boarding school, especially after lights-out, guys roughed each other up a lot. Only if it left marks or got loud enough to wake the dorm warden did adults get involved.

People were now heading into the school building en masse, and a glance at my phone told me the bell would ring soon. I followed Gina through the crowd and down the hall to our homeroom, where I got to open my locker, put my things in it, and slam it shut.

Okay, maybe it was sad that stuff like this made my day, but it did. That feeling I was in a teen movie was back.

Mr. Martinez was working at his desk and glanced up to smile as I put my report in his inbox. I'd been worried last night that Cassie might not have a printer, but she did down in her studio. It had even been stocked with paper.

As the clatter of the bell ringing made everyone pause and wince, I noticed that Amy hadn't arrived. It wasn't all that noteworthy until the next bell rang and everyone was taking their seats in the neat, utilitarian rows of desks. Gina was also frowning at her friend's empty desk. Then she grabbed her phone and scanned the screen.

With an uneasy look in my direction, she got up and walked to Mr. Martinez's desk, where he was still tapping away at his keyboard.

I slipped out of my seat to follow her.

"Mr. Martinez," she said, phone still in hand.

"Hmm? Yes?" He looked up.

Gina paused a moment, then held the phone out so he could read the screen. "It's Amy," she said.

His eyebrows lifted. "All right. You and Liana are excused. Go help her."

"Wait," I said as Gina turned around. "What's happened?"

9

*A*my was in the same bathroom I'd cowered in the day before, cowering in that same corner. I could hear her hiccuping sobs the moment Gina pushed open the door. "Aim?" she called.

She didn't answer, only kept crying.

I hung back, feeling like an intruder, while Gina rushed over and knelt on the floor in front of the stall.

Now that I wasn't the emotional wreck I'd been the day before, I noticed how much filth and grossness a person had to ignore to be willing to kneel or sit on the scuffed and dirty floor. Had I really sat on it yesterday? And Corban had too.

Where was Corban, anyway? I hadn't seen him in homeroom, but he hadn't been there yesterday either.

Amy was fumbling with the latch on the stall door. It swung open to reveal her looking like a wreck. Her face was puffy and swollen, her eyes bloodshot and tears still rolling down her cheeks.

I grabbed a paper towel and handed it to her, unsure of what else to do. She accepted it with a brief flash of a smile and blew her nose.

Gina put her arms around her friend. "You okay?" she asked.

I was too self-conscious to echo the question. It was obvious that Amy wasn't okay.

"Yeah. I don't know why it's so hard today, but it is." She looked past Gina, at me.

I wanted to disappear. There was no way she wanted me here while she was having this moment.

But she didn't give me a dismissive sneer. Instead she wiped her nose again and said, "My uncle was murdered a few years ago and… it's hard, you know? Maybe your situation triggered the memory, and I'm sorry… I don't mean to make it all about me."

"No, you're fine," I said. "I'm really sorry to hear that." It was hard not to gape at her. She had a family member who had been murdered too? I'd never met anyone else who could say that.

"And I guess I'm sorry that I don't know what it's like to have a family member murdered?" said Gina.

Amy laughed at that, actually laughed.

"Do you want to talk about your uncle?" I ventured.

"He was shot by his friend while they were both drunk," she said. "And his friend committed suicide the next day." She wiped her eyes. "Something similar happened to my cousin, who killed himself after he got in a car accident that killed his cousin. I mean, the problem is, once you start crying over this stuff, it's hard to stop. There's just so much of it."

I tried to wrap my head around what she was saying.

"Yeah, I have two cousins who died by suicide," said Gina.

"I... um... wow..." It was hard to string a sentence together when there were no words. I knelt down on the floor.

Amazingly, Amy reached out to me and the three of us hugged. I hadn't been hugged by another girl ever in my life. Feeling their arms around me had all the calming benefits of being held by Evan without any of the complications, and for the first time since I'd arrived in Taos, I felt the knots of stress in my heart begin to unravel.

Amy's rib cage shuddered as she took a deep breath. "Thanks, guys. I don't know why today was so much harder."

"Do you want to go to the nurse's office?" Gina asked her.

"Um, yeah, I think I will for a little while." She pulled some toilet paper off the roll and blew her nose in it.

"Okay, we'll walk with you." Gina got to her feet and helped us up to ours, giving my hand a warm, friendly squeeze.

As we walked back to class after dropping Amy off at the nurse's office, I asked, "So... is the suicide and murder rate really high here?"

The halls were empty, save for the buzzing of the lights and sound of people pushing desks around in one of the classrooms, so we kept our voices low.

"Mmm... I dunno," she said. "The stuff Amy was talking about happened in Espa."

"Espa?" I asked.

"Española. It's a town, like, between here and Santa Fe and that's where Amy's uncle and cousin were living. Her uncle married a woman from San Ildefonso Pueblo."

"Oh." For some reason, finding out that the uncle and cousin were father and child made the story even sadder. I looked down at the scuffed gray tile on the floor for a few steps. Then I remembered to say, "I'm really sorry about your cousins, too."

She shrugged. "One of them was deep in drug debt, and the drugs didn't help his mental state either. The other had just lost custody of his kid."

These were difficult issues, and not entirely foreign to me. If someone from the Hamptons lost custody, though, they could afford the legal fees to fight it. If they had an expensive drug habit that ran through their fortune, they often had wealthy family members who could swoop in and send them to expensive rehab.

I'd always known that with wealth came power and privilege, and that I'd won one of the most unfair lotteries in the universe. I'd been born with massive amounts of money, and that in turn had bought me opportunities at the best schools. My foray into Taos High made me a tourist, gawking at the lives of people from an utterly different world.

This hallway we walked down had plain white paint on the walls that had been scuffed and smudged, probably over the course of a decade or more. Some of the lights overhead flickered and a couple were burned out. It wasn't built this way to copy a teen movie, either. It was what the city could afford, and if someone wanted to study something offbeat, like ancient

Sumerian, no wealthy family foundations would front the money for a new teacher and a new section in the library. Life here was limited in ways I'd never truly experienced before.

"I'm sorry about your dad," said Gina.

"Thanks."

"Can I ask what happened?"

"We're not sure. He was shot through a window of our house with a sniper rifle, and the police are still trying to figure out who did it."

"Holy cow… that's crazy. Did they steal stuff?"

"No, which is what's kind of odd. They didn't come into the house at all. The police think it may be someone who has some kind of vendetta against him personally, and that's why they sent me here."

"The police did?"

I nodded. "I mean, they told me to come here, and to stay off the grid. I took a bus cross-country, so that there would be no record of me booking a flight, and, like, I can't withdraw money from my bank accounts or use my old credit cards. I had to get a new phone. If you have Facebook or Instagram or anything, don't post any pictures of me." I'd expected to have to say this sooner, but nobody had pointed a camera at me since I'd arrived.

"Did you have to delete your social media accounts?" Gina asked.

"No… I never had any. It helps that I was a boring person."

Gina cracked up. "Oh yeah, sooo dull."

It took me a second to realize that she thought I was being sarcastic, and once I did, I was too flattered to correct her. It also occurred to me that it was pretty insensitive to talk about not being able to access my money. I had enough on my prepaid credit card to keep me in comfort for a good long time. But Gina didn't seem to take offense or even notice.

I supposed my dad being murdered acted as a great equalizer. No amount of money would ever fill the void that had taken up residence right by my heart. The pain hadn't lessened, and I was beginning to suspect that it never would. I might get used to it and figure out how to go on in spite of it, but it would always be there.

"So, do you want to come to Amy's on Sunday to make tamales?" Gina asked. "Her mom works double shifts on Saturday, so that's kind of the only day."

"Oh, what's her mom do?"

"When she's not in the senate, she's a nurse."

"Senate?"

"Yeah, she's a state senator, but our state legislature only meets for a month or two out of the year. It's a lay legislature."

I'd never heard of such a thing.

"You want to come, though?" Gina repeated.

"I have no idea how to make a tamale," I confessed.

"No, it's easy. They'll give you one step to do and that's all you have to figure out."

"I don't want to intrude. Isn't it to welcome her brother home?"

"Why would you be intruding?" Gina looked at me like I was crazy. "You're her friend."

I was? After one day? That was fast, and it caught me so much by surprise that my throat went tight. *Don't cry,* I ordered myself. *Do. Not. Cry.*

"That a yes?" Gina pressed me.

I nodded. "Um… yeah. The only thing is, I really want to go to church." Not only was this part of my weekly ritual, I felt in especial need of it in my current condition. But I knew it was also incredibly straightlaced and not normal for most teenagers.

"You can come with me. I'm going beforehand. Catholic church."

"You are?"

She nodded, as if this, too, was perfectly normal.

There were other religious kids at the Hawke Academy, but few of them had been Christians. The ones who'd regularly gone to services and such were almost always Jewish or Muslim. Then again, I was deep in Catholic country.

"Um, yeah, that'd be great."

"Cool, and that way we can go straight to Amy's after." Gina flashed me a smile.

At lunchtime, there was a thunderstorm over the mountains, or perhaps a thunder snowstorm? The weather forecast called for snow this week, and through the panoramic windows of the cafeteria was this amazing view of dark clouds shooting bolts of lighting, followed a few seconds later by the sound of rolling thunder. If someone showed me a video of what I was staring at, I'd have thought that it was fake.

I gawked at it while my plate of tacos got cold and didn't even notice until Gina and Amy plonked themselves down across from me at the table.

"This view is amazing," I said.

They both looked and nodded, but it clearly wasn't anything special to them. People in my wealth bracket spent small fortunes to see such a view on vacation, and my friends were so used to having it for free that it wasn't worth a second look.

I did tear myself away from the view to look at Amy, though, who still looked a little fragile, but her tearstains had cleared up. For a moment I debated asking her how she was. Would that be annoying to her or comforting?

"So how are you?" Gina asked for both of us.

"Better," said Amy. "I don't know why it was so hard today. I mean, I woke up feeling the same as ever, but on the ride here I couldn't get my mind off how sad I was. It was like... I dunno. I looked to see if it was, like, the anniversary of either of their deaths or something, but it's not. Man, I feel like I'm shouting. It's so loud in here."

The cafeteria was louder than yesterday, now that she mentioned it. It was as if everyone had excess energy. They yelled, laughed extra loud, drummed on tables and strutted around even to do mundane things like take their tray over to the trash.

I sat up straighter and scanned the crowd more carefully. "Is Corban not here today?" I asked.

"Oh, I dunno," said Amy.

"I don't think I have any classes with him," said Gina.

"Yeah, me neither."

I looked at my friends. "He's not in our homeroom?" I asked.

Amy squinted, thinking that over. "Maybe? He's so quiet."

"Yeah, okay," said Gina. "He's in our homeroom. But yeah, he's quiet."

"But he gave you a ride home yesterday, right?" said Amy.

"Yeah, He and I got to talking. Just talking," I stressed.

Gina giggled. "He is totally hot, but like… what's the male version of an ice princess? An ice prince?"

"Ice princess is a sexist term anyhow," said Amy. She bit into one of her tacos and somehow managed not to get shredded lettuce and ground beef everywhere.

"Royal personage of a cool demeanor?" Gina suggested.

"Mmm, I like that," Amy said with her mouth full.

"So you guys don't know him at all?" I asked. I looked at my own tacos dubiously, then tried to watch Amy out of the corner of my eye. She turned each taco flat, so that she was eating it like a sandwich, rather than tilting her head to bite it at an angle. I gave that a try and managed to also not get the filling all over myself, and I was way happier about that than I would ever admit.

"No," said Gina. "I mean, everyone kind of knows him. He's really nice. He's sat at my table before, at our table, at lunch sometimes. He doesn't say much."

"Everyone likes him," said Amy. "A lot of girls more than like him."

"What's his family like?" I asked.

"He doesn't have one," said Gina. "He got orphaned... I don't know when."

Amy paused mid-chew, then shrugged and shook her head.

"I mean, he wasn't, like, real young," said Gina. "But it also wasn't super recent."

"So he's an emancipated minor?" I asked.

"I... don't know," said Gina. "He may be older than eighteen. I think maybe when his parents died, he took some time off school?"

The small towniness of Taos was paying off. Even people who "didn't know" Corban knew a lot. "What did they die of?"

"Car accident, I think," said Amy. "Way too common around here."

"Too many drunk drivers," Gina agreed.

"So where does he live? He doesn't have family around here?"

"He lives in the apartment complex near here. Tierra something apartments," said Amy.

I looked from her to Gina and back again. "Do you think he's a narc?"

"Maybe." Gina chuckled. "I mean, I don't know, but a lot of people think maybe. Except that, like, no one's been busted for drugs here in... I dunno how long."

"No one?" Not even the Hawke Academy could boast that. Aside from the supercompetitive kids abusing Adderall, there were students who dabbled in things like meth and ecstacy and got expelled over it.

"No one," said Amy. "That's part of why my parents wanted me to go here. My brothers all went to Indian boarding schools, but here is a better environment."

The page I'd written about Corban in my journal felt like it was burning through my wallet, trying to eat its way out of my bag like acid. There was too much about him that didn't add up.

A woman who I didn't recognize, but my friends did, approached the table. "Hi, Amy. How are you feeling?" she asked. She was older than most of my teachers with loose, age-spotted skin, but wore a faculty badge and had the air of a teacher. I could easily imagine her shouting at everyone in the cafeteria to keep it down.

"I'm okay," said Amy. "Liana, this is Mrs. Q, the school counselor."

"Oh, hi," I said.

"So this is Liana. Hi. Okay, I want both of you to come to group this afternoon. I'll excuse you from your next period."

Amy nodded.

So I did too.

Only after she left did I ask, "What's group?"

Gina gave me a pitying smile.

10

"Group" referred to group therapy in the counselor's office. It was me, Amy, and four other students, two of whom were pregnant. Another wore an ankle monitor that I stared at. This person was on parole from prison? It was a guy who was probably younger than I was.

We sat in chairs set out in a circle that included Mrs. Q, who gave everyone a warm smile. "All right, so this is Liana Linacre. Liana, you don't need to share any details. We'll just say that you're mourning a family member."

"My father," I said.

Everyone in the circle nodded.

"Ashley and Darcy, here, are in their third trimesters. Darcy's trying to decide whether to give her baby up for adoption. Carlos here has his hearing date coming up. He's been in the country for four years."

So he wasn't a criminal? He was an immigrant of some kind? What kind of immigrants wore ankle monitors?

"Lex, here, has an eating disorder."

Lex shrugged. "My family can't afford much food."

"They could if your father wasn't a drunk," said one of the pregnant girls.

"Hey, now," said the councillor. "No judgment."

"I'm not judging him. Just his dad."

And the discussion was off. As out of my element as I felt sitting with this group, I felt even more so talking to them. Lex's family was so deep in poverty that they were about to become homeless. Ashley was pregnant after being raped by her older sister's ex-boyfriend while she was visiting her in college. Darcy was thinking about putting her baby up for adoption because she was only fourteen, and her mother was thirty, so this was a cycle in her family.

And their stories were only the tip of the iceberg. They talked about cousins who were in prison, parents who'd died in drug overdoses, and a shockingly high number of suicides among their friends and extended families.

A week ago, I would have admitted I was a sheltered person. I knew that, but I also thought I knew the extent of my shelteredness. I thought I understood, at least intellectually, what it was like for the rest of the country.

Now I felt ripped from the shelter and thrust into the storm, and even as I felt this, I knew I was *still* sheltered. I was here in New Mexico for a few months, for an extended field trip into the rural southwest before I went back to New England for more fancy schooling on another wealth-endowed campus. These students would stay here, in this place, dealing with real life.

When I got home that afternoon after school, I got onto the internet and began reading, and a short time later I had my head down, body shaking with a mix of shock, horror, disbelief, and I hope a little compassion. It was hard to tell with all the shock, horror, and disbelief pulsing through me.

I'd made the mistake of looking up New Mexico's suicide and homicide statistics. My new home state had a slightly higher murder rate than my old home state–and I'd always thought of New York as a violent place. Its downward trend in homicides mirrored what I thought was a national trend. Taos looked so idyllic and removed from all that.

It was just a look, though. New Mexico was in the top five states for suicides, while New York was forty-ninth. Here in the isolated high desert, people were ending their lives at a rate that beggared belief. My friends and the other members of group therapy weren't alone when it came to the carnage of human suffering.

That also made it extra strange that the high school had little to no drug use and a history of no fights.

I WENT TO school the next day with my eyes open. The feeling I was in a fun teen movie had evaporated completely, and it felt like my first full day in the real world.

The guy who sat in front of me in homeroom had a nervous twitch, and later I heard his father would sometimes call him from prison during school hours. There was a girl in my chemistry class who never made eye contact and had marks on her inner forearms from a razor blade. There were students who'd gotten so little sleep that their eyes looked bruised, and students who wore ragged, faded clothes because they couldn't even afford to restock their wardrobe from WalMart.

There were other students who were undocumented, including one girl in my math class who had been shipped north by her family in Guatemala after her brother was murdered there. Who was I to feel bad about losing my father when there were people in the world who carried that kind of grief and had no safe place to run in their entire country? There was the guy in history who had only just learned he wasn't an American citizen because his parents had carried him across the border when he was a baby. He planned to join the military after high school, and I hadn't even realized noncitizens could do that. Gina assured me it wasn't uncommon.

And Carlos, I finally figured out, wore an ankle monitor because he'd arrived in the US on his own at sixteen but had lied about his age and said he was eighteen. Then, later, when he figured out he was allowed to go to school until he was twenty-one, he copped to his actual age, but was eighteen by then and still had to wear the monitor.

It wasn't just big things that threw me for a loop either. There were a million little things. Most of my classmates, I learned, hadn't even signed up to take the SAT, and few of them applied to any colleges for early admission. There was a small cadre of high-performing students, but most people who were working on applications now were applying for associates programs.

The guidance office in the school fought against a heavy burden of history and heritage. There were maybe a dozen students applying to the Ivy League– Amy was in that group. Her mother had a degree from Dartmouth, it turned out, but many families in the region had gone for generations without sending anyone to college. My family, as far back as I knew, didn't have a generation that *hadn't* sent someone to college. All of the boys up until the nineteen fifties, and both genders after that.

I learned via eavesdropping that students went home to houses without running water or electricity, to parents who were abusive, to families who were illiterate, and that didn't count all the students who went from school straight to work. I overheard one girl in the cafeteria talking about how she'd taken on a third job and didn't get home until after one in the morning.

Corban again didn't show for homeroom and I didn't get any glimpses of him for the rest of the day. I had his phone number, of course, but I didn't feel like I could call him. He was an acquaintance at most, a guy who'd conned me into having some insane conversations at worst. In spite of that, or perhaps because of it, I missed him. I wanted to talk to him. He was almost as much of a friend as Gina and Amy were.

All of these thoughts were washing over me while I sat in the cafeteria at lunch, so I didn't hear Amy until she said, "Liana?" in the sing-songy voice that signalled it wasn't the first time she'd tried to get my attention.

"Hmm? Sorry, what? Sorry," I said.

Gina was also staring at me. "Can I just ask you, is this your usual level of spaciness? Or is something up?"

"I'm just overwhelmed," I explained, before taking a bite of my burrito. The cafeteria had served burritos today, and I'd only ever had the gourmet kind from a truck that parked near the beach in Southampton. These had fewer ingredients, but still tasted amazing. Once I'd chewed and swallowed, I tried to put my thoughts into words. "I'm having a rich girl's crash course in real life."

"What do you mean?" asked Amy.

How to explain without being a jerk about it? "I'm from a world where people can buy their way out of a lot of the problems people here deal with."

"Oh," said Gina. "Yeah, well, real problems affect everyone, even people with money. You still lost your father. Rich people deal with heartbreak and disappointment and pain just like anyone else."

"But we don't," I said. "And it's not fair. I'll probably never know what it's like to wonder where I'm gonna live and what I'm gonna eat tomorrow."

"Me neither," said Gina.

"Yeah, me neither," said Amy, "and I totally qualify as poor. As for having enough food, I was asking if you wanted to come make tamales on Sunday at my house."

"And I was telling her I'd already invited you," said Gina. "And you were all staring off into space for so long I was starting to wonder if we had to search you for medic alert jewelry."

"Sorry."

"Yeah, you said that," replied Gina. "About fifty times."

I looked around the cafeteria. It was noisy again today, and there was an edge to the rabble. Like tempers were wearing thin and truces were about to break. "Is Corban often gone from school for days at a time?"

Amy and Gina both considered that, and both shrugged.

"I don't have a crush on him," said Gina, "so I don't watch his every move."

"Me neither," said Amy. "Why, do you?"

I shook my head. "No. Nothing like that. We just had some stuff in common. Like, he sorta knew a friend of mine from back east." *You are sounding lame,* I told myself.

But my friends didn't laugh at me.

"I'm sure he'll be back tomorrow," said Gina. "I don't think he goes away for very long, ever."

RATHER THAN GO to my next class, I got summoned to the counselor's office again, but this time there was no ring of chairs and no trial-by-fire of real life waiting for me. Only Mrs. Q wearing a concerned look. "Liana," she said, after sitting me down in a chair on the other side of her desk, "I wanted to ask you about your aunt. When you didn't talk about her yesterday in group, I assumed you didn't want to."

"Cassie?" I shrugged. "I'm not ashamed of her or anything. I mean… I know she's a little bizarre."

"How has she been?"

"I'm not sure. I didn't see her last night." After recovering from my internet search, I'd worked on homework and couldn't even remember if I heard her shuffling around downstairs. She hadn't come up to the kitchen.

"I see. How much do you know about her?" Mrs. Q's gaze was a mix of empathy and unease.

"Um…" I said, "Not much, really." Dread was building in the pit of my stomach. There was only so much reality I could take, and I had the sinking feeling I was about to take on more.

"Sooo," said Mrs. Q, "it's been a while, but she has… incidents sometimes."

I bit my lip, then asked, "What kind of incidents?"

"Well… she got arrested a few years ago for walking around downtown and screaming obscenities at people for no reason."

"Oh," I said.

"And she's been in treatment. I don't know for what, but Lydia was looking after her house for a while."

"You know Lydia?" I asked. "The chef?" Even though Taos was small, it surprised me that the school counselor knew someone who lived out in my aunt's subdivision by her first name.

"Yeah, she's Red Willow."

"Okay," I said. "What does that mean?"

"Taos Pueblo are the Red Willow People."

"Oh."

"And I'm from the pueblo. I mean, I married in. My husband is Red Willow. My last name is actually Quotskuvya, but that's a mouthful."

"Yeah… It is."

"Lydia's kind of a career house sitter. Rich people with multiple houses trust her to water their plants and feed their horses and stuff."

I absorbed that. "So does Lydia cook for my aunt to… to help take care of her?"

"I don't know. Cassie pays her well, so it helps Lydia a lot. I only know Cassie because she buys dyes from my daughter-in-law, so we see her every week, but she didn't show up yesterday for her usual pickup. It doesn't necessarily mean anything and it's happened before. If you're living with her, though, you should be aware."

I got out my phone and called my aunt. The call went to voicemail, which wasn't necessarily concerning. It was possible that she was engrossed in dying wool. Except that according to Mrs. Q, she'd be low on dye.

"I'll make sure to check on her this afternoon," I promised.

WHEN I WALKED up to the house from the bus stop that afternoon, though, I found the house door open and all the lights off inside. "Cassie?" I called out.

No answer.

11

For a long moment all I could do was stare at the open door, my insides quaking. If only Dad were around. He knew his sister. He grew up with her. Besides, if he were here, I would be living with him and not going it alone in an Earthship with a nominal guardian who was de facto weird.

Grief pierced my heart. Could I even do this anymore? Maybe it would be best if I got my own apartment and got on with my life. Except I didn't want to be alone and I didn't want to be without the one member of my family that I had left. Why couldn't Cassie have it together? Why couldn't she be there for me? Why couldn't Dad's death mean that I got to mourn while she supported me? Wasn't that how this kind of thing was supposed to work?

Maybe all Cassie had done today was leave the door open, but what if she hadn't? What if she was having some form of meltdown? What gave her the right to do that, and why couldn't it be me instead? Why couldn't it be her standing outside the door to my room, agonizing over how to be there for me and make sure I was okay?

Hot tears spilled out of my eyes, and I rubbed them away with my knuckles. Shame bubbled up, but I pushed it away with an almost physical force. I was an orphan. I'd lost everything. I'd had my blood sucked and my life taken from me. I could cry if I wanted to.

But I also had to check on Cassie. With a resigned straightening of my spine, I went inside.

I found my aunt seated on the stairs, still in her bathrobe, clasping her head like it was about to explode. Despite the huge windows on the south side of the house, her posture made the place feel dim and even a little closed in.

I was so far out of my depth that I approached with caution. Helpless didn't even begin to describe how I felt.

"Cassie?" I ventured again while I came down the stairs to where she was. My mind raced with desperation. What was I supposed to do if she needed serious help of some kind?

I made myself take a breath and think. Cassie had lived on her own for years. Whatever this was, she would know what to do if I could only get her to talk. Or I hoped she would.

And perhaps I was overreacting. Perhaps I'd taken Mrs. Q's comments too much to heart and was blowing the situation out of proportion. Leaving a door open didn't have to be a sign of a serious problem. She was an artsy, absent-minded person, and Taos seemed like the kind of place that was overrun with people who'd leave their doors open because their minds were elsewhere.

These thoughts calmed me down some as I sat down on the stair beside her.

"Hey," I said. "Do you need anything?"

Her only reply was a gasping noise, as if she was fighting the urge to hyperventilate.

Be cool, I ordered myself. I didn't know what else to say, so I didn't talk.

She continued to gasp, and then began to breathe long, shaky breaths. After several of these, she lifted her head and stared toward the south windows. From where we sat we had a clear view of the flat expanse of desert. There were other Earthship houses out there, but they either blended in or were hidden by land features. The dirt roads crisscrossing the scene was the only evidence of other inhabitants.

"You can tell me to go away," I said. "I just want to make sure I'm not… disrupting your life somehow?"

"I need disruption," she said. She took another deep breath.

"Okay… Um, Mrs. Q at school asked me to check on you–"

"Because I've got severe obsessive-compulsive disorder."

"Oh," I said. "Okay."

"And I was getting so good at not obsessing. At laughing at the little voices in my head that tell me I have to do this or I have to touch that. I was getting good at doing whatever I wanted."

"I never would have thought you were OCD," I agreed.

She shot me a look laced with wry humor. "Just crazy?"

"In a good way," I said, with an awkward shrug.

"Your father used to call me a kook. Did he ever tell you that?"

"Can I plead the fifth?"

She chuckled. "I never did tell your dad about my condition. Or our parents."

That was a big secret to have to carry around, and I knew a thing or two about that. "Is there anything you need?" I asked. "Or is this, sitting here, what you need?" That much I could do.

"I need to find my happy place again. I need to feel like I'm thumbing my nose at the demons that tell me that if I don't go touch certain objects in a certain order, terrible, evil things will happen. I need to not care that my brain is built to melt down if I don't close the door exactly right. I need to feel like I can push through any panic attack, and just keep living while alarm bells are blaring inside and my heart's beating like it's going to bust out of my chest."

What I wouldn't give for superpowers like that. She could do these things? It gave me a twisted kind of hope. Maybe I could learn to find happiness while my heart was breaking and the tempest inside me continued to rage.

She laughed, then. "You're the real kook, Liana. You leave New York to live out here and you find out your guardian is mentally ill and lives mid-panic attack all the time and you're just like, 'Cool, okay. That's fine.'"

I wasn't fine, but I guess I hid it well. "Maybe I'm like you," I said. "Everything that's happened since I came here hasn't made me feel any better about Dad's death, but it's distracting. I'm kind of dividing my mind. Part of me is doing okay, and part of me is in pain. Like, constant, unbearable, horrible pain." Just acknowledging it made my throat close up.

She nodded. "Yeah, I feel that too. I barely ever talked to my brother, but I miss him so much. I mean, *so* much. I want to ask you about him and what he was like all these years, but I don't want to go into that pain and I don't want to take you there. I try to divide my mind and make a space for myself where I can mourn without having the little voices interfere, but it doesn't always work."

My chest was tightening and tears were forming in my eyes. I forced myself to breathe, and realized I was doing exactly what Cassie was doing moments ago, and for some completely irrational, insane reason, that made me laugh. "Think there's a medical definition for what we do, dividing our minds?" I asked, a hysterical edge to my voice. "It's kind of like retreating to one room of the house while the rest is on fire, isn't it?"

"Maybe that's what you do," she said. "I go farther. I throw a party in that room, crank up the music, play dress up, and dance like a maniac."

"That is totally a superpower."

"Yeah, well, I always thought so. For the past two days, though, I haven't eaten. I haven't dyed wool. I disrupt my routine on purpose all the time to prove to myself that I can, but it never goes this long."

"Well, do you want me to make sure you get fed?" I asked. "Or do you want to talk to your doctor, or what?"

She took another deep breath. "I should talk to my therapist. I just hate it. It's not like I don't know what's wrong. My brother died, and his daughter is here, and I'm worried I'll screw this up."

"You're fine, Aunt Cassie. You've done so much for me. What's your therapist's number?"

"Well… give me ten minutes, okay? If in ten minutes I don't come up the stairs, my therapist's number is on the fridge. Call it then?"

"Okay," I agreed.

Walking back upstairs was still nerve-wracking, though. I didn't know what I was doing at all. I was winging it with no more knowledge of how to help someone with OCD than the trite conclusions portrayed on television and in the movies. The only reason I was still functioning in this new reality I'd been thrust into was because I was in so much shock, it hadn't all sunk in yet.

So I was very, *very* relieved when Aunt Cassie came up the stairs a few minutes later and called her therapist. While she spoke, I retreated into my room and wished I had someone to talk to. There was no way I could dump this stuff on Gina or Amy, and Corban… Corban was gone. He had been around for exactly one day, then disappeared.

Cassie talked on the phone for almost half an hour. After she hung up, she came to the door of my room, where I was seated on my bed, jotting down notes for chemistry (not having my own book meant no highlighting. It also meant I'd ordered my own copy from Amazon and could not wait for it to arrive.)

"Liana, can we talk about your comment about vampires?" she asked.

That hit like a ton of bricks. All the residual embarrassment I felt from a couple of days ago came crashing down. Still, she'd owned her crazy to me. I owed her.

"Is there a mental illness that makes people think they're vampires?" I asked.

"Yeah. It could be a psychotic delusion–"

"Whoa," I said. "Psychotic? Like I'm an axe murderer?"

She shook her head. "Psychotic means you have intense delusions that you can't distinguish from reality. Like people who have imaginary friends that they don't know are imaginary."

"Oh…" Was Corban imaginary? The school secretary had introduced him to me and I'd seen Amy and Aunt Cassie talk to him. Surely he wasn't...

"Or it could be some form of body dysmorphia," said my aunt.

Despite my private school education, I could not handle all the Latin terms she was flinging around. "Do you think I'm crazy?" I asked.

"No. I don't. You're too boring."

I wasn't sure how to respond to that, so I just looked at her.

"And not in that morose way," she added. "You aren't all shut into your own world. You have friends and you talk to people and you always seem lucid. So I'm a little confused about why Corban was praying in your room the other day and you made some strange comment about vampires."

"I'm confused too," I confessed. "And I'm not sure I want to tell anyone what was going on because I don't know what to think about it myself and–"

"You sound like you're an abuse victim," she said. "Something's eating at you and you don't feel like you can share it because you're afraid people will laugh."

"Pretty sure people will either laugh or want to lock me up," I said.

"Again, you sound like an abuse victim." She leaned against my door frame.

Her point was valid, but so was mine.

Nevertheless, she was my guardian, or at least she was the person giving me a home and shelter until I went to college. She had a right to know what was going on.

Never had I found it so hard to be the good girl. I was used to living my truth despite what the world thought. I was the boring nerd, and I was good with that. All my little jealousies about not dating or being prettier had paled in comparison to the pride I'd felt in knowing myself and not being afraid of it.

Never had I considered that some people couldn't embrace their truth because they couldn't accept it. Because it was too painful or too strange or the social cost of putting it out there was so astronomical. I'd stupidly thought that being a nerd was one of the hardest truths to live.

And now, maybe, the universe was teaching me a lesson.

12

In slow, halting sentences, I told my aunt the truth. The story I hadn't been able to make myself tell Corban came out line by cringeworthy line.

And through it all, Cassie listened, leaning against my door frame, gaze attentive and nonjudgmental. My respect for her went up many, many notches.

Once I'd finished, she chewed the inside of her lip a moment, then said, "I'm thinking maybe hypnosis. People can be talked into pretty strange stuff with post-hypnotic suggestion."

"They can?" I asked.

She nodded. "Yeah, so it is theoretically possible that this is an implanted delusion. The sunrise thing, that could also be post-hypnotic suggestion."

"Okay, so what is that?"

"It's a technique where you hypnotize a person and…" She waved her hand vaguely for a moment. "Implant a trigger? Like stage hypnotists will tell people that when they hear a certain word, they'll do a certain action, like strut around like a chicken."

"That was on *Fuller House*," I said. "Kimmie did the chicken thing when–"

"Yeah," said Cassie, "it was on *Fuller House*. As a joke. But I've had hypnotherapy and it's helped me resist my compulsions. The hypnotist… I can't really explain it in technical terms because I don't know them, but basically he makes it so that when a panic attack starts, I also get this feeling that I can handle it. It's like he tells my subconscious to help me out while it's also beating the crap out of me."

"So Evan could have hypnotized me and made me believe that he was drinking my blood and stuff."

"Right. Maybe. I don't know. Possibly."

"And implanted the pain I feel every sunrise? Made sunrise the trigger?"

She nodded. "It's a *guess*, okay? I may be a kook, but I'm not some whacko who believes in vampires."

"Hey, if you have a theory that I can look up in a medical journal, I am totally on board. So how do we find out if that's what I've got? Talk to your hypnotist?"

She shrugged. "Yeah… I think maybe asking him generally, but there's a problem with that theory. Corban. He corroborated the vampire thing."

"Right." I flopped back on my bed. "Unless I hallucinated the conversation I had with him? Like I had a trigger–"

"Unlikely," said Cassie. "That's going pretty far beyond what a hypnotist can do. Somehow you had a conversation that ended up with him coming here and doing his ritual thingy."

"So what do you think is going on with me?"

"Either that there's a cult out there that has ninja hypnosis skills and an extensive membership that includes the local Boy Scout heartthrob, or I don't know," she said. "And here I've got to tell you something. I can't help you deal with this. I'm sorry. I can give you my hypnotist's phone number but–"

"You're fine," I said. I'd never expected adults to fix my problems. That was the thing about being a boarding school kid. I was used to dealing with things on my own. All I wanted was emotional support now and then.

"I have to look after me," she said. "And that means putting my full energy into being irresponsible, because irresponsible me–"

"Can resist the demons that try to control you," I said. "Fight an illness that increases a person's odds of suicide by a factor of ten. I know. I Googled."

"But if you need a real adult," she said, "I can see what I can do."

"I've got to hide out from whoever killed my dad," I said. "We still don't know who it was or why they did it. I was thinking maybe I should go live somewhere on my own."

"No," she answered. "You don't handle stuff like this all on your own. If you're okay here dealing with your issues while I deal with mine, then stay. All right?"

It wasn't an ideal solution, but it was the best on offer. I nodded. "Okay. So we have a mutual pact that if we see the other self-destructing, we try to do something or tell someone or…"

"Right," she said. "No guarantees, just a promise to try if we can."

"Got it." And even though it sounded like a precarious position, I suspected it was better than what a lot of people had.

AFTER A GOOD two hours of internet research, though, I was pretty sure my condition hadn't been implanted by post-hypnotic suggestion. It also didn't seem to be a delusion. There was just too much corroborating evidence. Either I was in a padded room somewhere, dreaming up this entire reality with Aunt Cassie and her Earthship and a mysterious boy who knew about vampires, or this was reality.

Being completely honest with myself, I wasn't that creative. Even deep in my subconscious, I wouldn't concoct such a story.

I pulled out my notes on Corban, my list of everything about him that didn't quite fit. This, I suspected, was wishful thinking. I was imagining a savior because I couldn't save myself. Pathetic.

It was hard to sleep that night. I lay as still as I could and did my best to ignore my rambling thoughts, even picturing my mind as a house and me retreating into a private room. I imagined Cassie being the source of all the noise, throwing her party and screaming banshee wails at the heavens to prove to herself that she could.

I must have eventually drifted off, because the next thing I knew was the flesh-peeling agony of sunrise. Tears spilling from my eyes didn't bring relief, and my prayers were mental screams of anguish.

When relief broke over me, I felt spent, like I'd just gone for a ten-mile run, not that I actually knew what that felt like. It took me a while before I could sit up.

Why? I wondered. *Why didn't I ask Corban whether I was beyond redemption?* I should have done it when I had the chance, rather than assuming I could later. If there was anyone else from his order in the area, I had no idea who they were.

I emerged from my room to find Cassie back to her kooky self, waltzing around the kitchen to her own, silent soundtrack. That made me feel a whole lot better. Whatever my issues, they hadn't pulled her down. I asked her if she'd eaten and she opened her mouth to show me her half-chewed granola, so I left for school feeling that my rapidly tilting world wasn't tilting quite as rapidly.

I counted that as a win. The promised snowstorm had arrived in the night, so there was a two-inch layer of snow on the ground that I walked through to the bus stop. It was as if the world had been born anew, and the air was crisp and cool and perfect.

But another day of school went by without Corban, and as much as I wanted to pretend I was okay with that, I wasn't.

Chaos continued to wrack the campus. Today two more people didn't show up to homeroom. One was found by friends cowering in the bathroom, the other appeared to have run away from home. A police officer was assigned to patrol the halls, and people acted like that was really unusual.

During lunch, another fight broke out and someone threw a chair, which hit and knocked over a table and sent trays and plates and drinks flying. Everyone near it scattered like it was a bomb, and the rest of us all packed ourselves up against the windows while the uniformed police officer called for backup. The two of them then tromped in and hauled the chair-flinger off.

The rest of the hour was unnaturally quiet as people picked at their food and tension sang in the air like the whine of a drill bit on metal.

None of this, I reminded myself, was out of the ordinary in a public high school in an economically depressed area, but everyone else was behaving like it was strange.

As I was packing up at my locker at the end of the day, Gina tugged on my elbow. "Help me study for tomorrow's quiz?" she begged. "If I get a B, my dad says I need to quit my apprenticeship."

"Yeah," I said, "of course." An afternoon of studying was my idea of fun, after all.

She drove me to her house, which had her jeweler's bench in the garage. It looked like she had to sit crammed between the wall and the bumper of the car behind her with only inches to spare. The scent of singed hair was very pungent against the scent of cold concrete and dust.

I stopped to gaze at her work, unable to help myself. Half-completed rings, earrings, and bracelets were scattered atop the bench, along with a bevy of tools I couldn't identify.

"No, don't look," she said. "I know it's all really bad."

I picked up a flat piece of silver that had been stamped with sinuous lines and was likely going to be a bracelet. "This is beautiful. I've never seen anything like it."

"It's… I'm a beginner, okay?" She clutched her backpack to her chest and stood, awkwardly, conveying that she really was embarrassed.

"I'm serious. It's beautiful."

"Thanks." She looked down. "Come on in."

I put down the bracelet and followed her into a house that was all rounded edges, probably because it was made out of real adobe. Even the corner where walls met was rounded, and I was getting used to that look. The floor was brick and the living room was sunken. A kiva fireplace dominated one wall and a cowskin rug covered the floor. The furniture was made of chunky wood and bright colored fabric–I knew people in the Hamptons who paid big money to decorate rooms like this. Here, though, it was considered normal. Given what I'd seen of furniture shops in town, it was probably hard to get pieces that didn't look like this.

Gina popped popcorn and we both folded open our netbooks. Tutoring her wasn't too difficult. She was smart enough, just crippled by anxiety. Once I got her to focus on the work, though, she got through it efficiently and we finished the assignment by the time her mother came home from work.

On the drive back to my house, Gina pointed to a block of stuccoed apartments and said, "That's where Corban lives. But I don't see his car."

I didn't either. There were no turquoise RAV4s parked in the lot.

The sun set along the way and Gina dropped me off at home with a grateful hug. I walked across the now frozen dirt which crunched a little under my boots (the snow had burned off during the day).

Inside, Aunt Cassie was sitting in the kitchen in the dark, her elbows on the table and her hands clutching each other. "Happy birthday," she said. "Sorry I didn't get you a cake."

I stopped dead in my tracks. It *was* my birthday, and I'd completely forgotten. If that wasn't a sign of how messed up my life had gotten, what was?

13

"It is your birthday, right?" Cassie asked.

"Yeah, thanks. You okay? Can I turn a light on?" I reached for the light switch.

"I'm okay," she said. "I'm more than okay."

"All right," I said. "I'm gonna turn this light on."

"Liana, please respect the fact that this is my house."

I withdrew my hand. "Yeah, sure. Um… I'll go to my room?"

"And I told you that you didn't have to check in with me!"

"Okay. I'm sorry."

"Will you just get out of here? I have a pounding headache."

"Okay…" I wasn't sure what else to say, so I went to my room and shut the door behind me, wondering how I would get dinner tonight. I didn't want to lie down to sleep while I was hungry. While I didn't know for a fact that this would make it harder to fight my vampirism, I didn't want to take any chances.

By opening my door a crack and peering out, I saw that Cassie was still there. "Can I get food?" I asked.

With an angry huff she stood up, knocking her chair over onto the floor, shot me a baleful look, and stalked off downstairs.

I was trying not to annoy her, but how could I avoid essential things like eating?

There were no leftovers in the fridge, which was a little odd because there'd been quite a bit left over yesterday. I poured myself a bowl of cereal, but I was worried I'd be hungry again in five minutes, so I toasted some Pop Tarts too, then I retreated into my room with my food so that I'd be out of the way if Cassie came back upstairs.

It was hard to just sit and eat, though. I wondered if my aunt was okay, or if I should call her therapist. Nevertheless, I made myself finish my cereal and half a Pop Tart before I went to the kitchen landing and called down, "Aunt Cassie?"

"What, Liana?" she snapped.

"Nothing. I just wondered–"

"Do not ask me if I'm okay."

Well, that didn't leave me with anything to ask her, so I hesitated a moment, then retreated, aware that I'd just made her more annoyed, but unsure of what to do about it.

Back in my room, I was at loose ends, but I knew if I stayed up and worried, I'd only risk turning vamp in the night, so I changed to my pajamas and didn't bother with brushing my teeth, because I had to go downstairs to the bathroom to do that and suspected that would only annoy her.

Tucking myself in bed, I shut my eyes and did my best to zone out.

Happy birthday to me. I was eighteen now, an adult. It was the birthday people usually celebrated the most, but mine had passed without so much as a lit candle or cupcake.

Or a phone call from my dad... If he were alive, he'd have woken me up with a call and said, "Many happy returns, Liana! You got time today to Skype?" He would have wanted to go over my financial accounts and reiterate the plan for what funds to use for college and whether or not I wanted to buy a place in New Jersey to live. He would have treated me with the businesslike air of a trusted advisor, rather than the gushing protectiveness of a doting father, but that was how my dad was, and the usual pang in my chest intensified until it felt like a stab wound.

Tears dripped onto my pillow while I forced myself to relax and let go into unconsciousness.

CORBAN'S CHUCKLE CUT across my thoughts and I jolted awake, eager to see him, but the room was empty. I sat up.

"Corban?" I rasped.

He wasn't here, nor had he been a moment ago.

I'd finally managed to fall asleep, only to get woken up by a dream.

I reached up to feel for my pulse in my neck, but froze before my fingers touched my skin. There was a mirror in the wall to my left that I only needed to roll over and look at, but I didn't.

If I wasn't still human, I wasn't ready to face it. Besides, if I saw that I was a vampire, what good would that do? I'd probably talk myself into running from sunrise in a few hours and then the world would have one more bloodsucking predator to deal with.

I stayed on my back and shut my eyes. Whether I was human or not, I had to believe that I was. I had to face sunrise without fear that I wouldn't survive it.

Again I heard Corban's chuckle, but I knew it was only in my mind. My imagination was in overdrive. I could imagine him sitting in the chair near the foot of my bed, arms folded, a smirk on his face. "Yeah," I heard him say. "You're not strong at all, are you?"

THE NEXT MORNING, I woke up to the feeling that two white-hot pokers were being jammed into my eye sockets, pinning my head to the pillow. It was the same kind of pain that I'd felt every sunrise, but worse.

A tight band of iron was around my rib cage, preventing me from breathing. Through the starburst explosions breaking across my field of non-vision, I was able to force one coherent thought through: I couldn't burn to ash and leave that for Aunt Cassie to find. She'd been through enough.

Molten metal wasn't just pouring over my skin. It poured straight through it to my bones.

I wanted to cry, but my eyes couldn't produce tears. That, I decided, was it, the sign that I'd turned and now I was going to die. My life and my mad flight away from my father's murder were going to end here and now, in a puff of smoke and then oblivion. Everything I'd fought for had come down to this.

Well, this wasn't nothing. I refused to be ashamed of what I'd accomplished. I'd held off vampirism for almost two weeks and trained myself to let the sun end me when…

Wait… I thought. My thoughts were too coherent. How could I think at all during this pain?

Except the pain had lessened. It still hurt like molten metal, but on the skin, not in my bones. It was as if I were being hollowed out, a shell of pain around an empty void. I could feel the event horizon expanding through my flesh until the void pushed its way out of me.

Tears streaked across my temples.

I was breathing too, but the short, clipped breaths that verged on hyperventilating. When I made myself breathe deeper, though, I did, and I could feel the air rushing into my lungs.

With my jaw set, I peeled one eye open and looked up at the skylight. I lifted one arm and my hand slid into my field of vision. Same hand as yesterday, no paler or ashier than before.

Okay, I thought, I can do this. I sat up and felt the vertebrae in my back pop as I did. Before I could stop myself, I turned to look at the mirror.

Same old me, or new me, I guess. I was still vampire pretty, but I had a reflection and my hair looked like I'd just come in from the rain.

Because of how much I'd sweated just now.

Don't get me wrong, I was relieved, but it was also pretty gross.

CASSIE WAS IN the kitchen, munching on a Pop Tart. "These are disgusting," she said. At least she was eating one of the old ones, not the new ones I'd bought. I'd forgotten to get rid of the faded box.

"They are disgusting," I agreed. "I don't think there's anything of any nutritional value in those."

"Probably just a lot of over-processed ingredients and chemicals. I may be taking a day off my life with each bite."

"You don't have to eat that. I'll make it disappear if you want."

"I made you eat these, so I'm doing my penance. Don't argue with me."

I filled the coffeemaker with grounds and water. "Who says you have to do penance?"

"Not the little voices in my head, if that's what you're worried about. This is all part of the house party, even has the colors to match." She held up what was left of the pink and white "pastry".

"Fair enough," I said.

"And I'm sorry about last night," she said.

"You're fine."

"I feel like I'm getting better, though. It's always like this, a roller coaster."

I nodded, glad that she was sounding lucid.

She finished her Pop Tart, poured herself a bowl of coffee, and stayed in the kitchen rather than going downstairs. I remembered what she said about breaking her own routines on purpose and decided that's what she was doing here.

This put me in a good mood a few minutes later as I walked through more new-fallen, powdery snow to the bus stop. It was at least three inches deep, but fortunately, the roads were visible as packed pathways, and the Earthships were so widely spaced that I could see the other girls waiting at the bus stop a block away.

There were two of them who got on with me, both younger, both quiet. They didn't greet me when I walked up, but they also weren't the kind that seemed to mean anything by that. One was listening to music on headphones and the other one was staring off at the snowcapped peaks in the distance. I looked up at the pale-gray sky and was grateful that even what little sun that filtered through was enough to burn the vampirism out of me.

At least my reality was peaceful in this moment. It was still a little washed out with grief and a little jagged with uncertainty, but I could credibly say I felt "fine." I concentrated on the refreshing feeling of inhaling lungfuls of chilled air and burying my hands in my warm, microfiber-lined pockets.

Except that the bus was taking a long time to come. It was five minutes late, and the other girls sure were glancing at their cell phones a lot. At ten minutes late, they started making calls to their parents. At eighteen minutes late, one of them got a call. "The bus isn't coming," she announced to us. "Something really, really bad happened."

14

A few bad things had happened, in fact. The bus hadn't come to get us because one student had stabbed another on board. Three days ago I'd boarded the bus like a wide-eyed kid at Disneyland, all wrapped up in the gleeful sense of living that American teen movie. The following day I'd figured out that was shallow and had noticed how many kids fell asleep, or glared at other bus-riders, or ate their lunch before school had even started.

Today, that bus full of real people with real lives had been required to make a detour to rendezvous with an ambulance to take a stabbing victim to the hospital, and a police cruiser to take a stabbing suspect into custody.

Right now, there was no word about the condition of the stabbee.

"Um, so my mom's gonna come give me a ride," said one of the girls. "You guys can come if you need."

The other girl nodded in a way that told me these two knew each other.

I thanked her and, for the third time this week, climbed into the car of a stranger. This time it was an aged SUV with cracked vinyl upholstery that had no trouble with the snow, and the driver was a kind, blond lady who knew my aunt.

We arrived at school about fifteen minutes late, and despite our perfectly valid excuse, we were all marked tardy.

Yet another reality that weighed on kids without reliable home lives or transportation. It took a few tardies to rack up a detention, but that still meant people sat in detention because of situations they couldn't control.

I also didn't see why we had to be penalized, because rather than going to class, everyone had been called into a last-minute assembly in the gym. There, people were seated by class in the bleachers, and Mr. Martinez's class was at the back, so it was pretty easy for me to slip into a seat on the hard bench beside Gina and behind Amy, whose jaw tensed in a slow rhythm as she chewed gum.

"–unacceptable behavior," the principal was saying when I arrived. "Someone here knows why this happened, and we're not leaving until they come forward. If you're too embarrassed to stand up right now, pass a note to your teacher and your teacher can let me know you're willing to talk. I don't want to be here all day, so start talking." Her face was somber, her gray hair pulled primly up in a bun and her slight figure commanding everyone's attention.

"How's the kid who got stabbed?" I whispered to Gina.

"Who got stabbed?" she whispered back.

She looked like she'd been paying attention to Principal Garcia, so I asked, "What's this assembly about?"

"The vandalism last night. A group of students broke into the library and tried to set it on fire."

"What?"

"But someone saw the flashlight beams and called the police and Principal Garcia is trying to shame us into giving up whoever did it."

I blinked. "Does stuff like this happen often?"

"No."

Amy leaned back to look up at me. "No," she also mouthed, shaking her head.

"And if they dust for prints," Gina said, "it'll look like a big ol' gang of the nerdiest kids over the past ten years did it."

I stifled a laugh at that. I would certainly have fit into that category at my old school.

"The world has gone crazy," Amy added.

Mr. Martinez had come a few steps down the aisle and made a shushing gesture at us.

I put my hands in my lap and pressed my lips together. I'd never been chided in an assembly before. It was rather exciting.

But I chastised myself for that thought. People trying to burn down the library was a big deal. I wondered if my friends had any suspicions, and now I couldn't ask because I'd blown our cover by giggling.

Gina didn't seem to think so, though. She leaned over to me. "I'm not sure if anyone here is sure who did it. I mean, we all have our guesses."

"How far did they get?" I asked.

"Tried to pry open the doors with a crowbar and wrecked the doors. Ran off leaving jugs of gasoline."

"I bet it was Estevan Marquez," said Amy. "He likes fire."

Mr. Martinez appeared in my peripheral vision again and I hunched my shoulders with guilt. Amy and Gina just looked at him as if to say, "This is ridiculous, and you know it."

"So who got stabbed?" Gina whispered to me.

"Um…" I still wasn't sure about flouting our teacher's authority. "Um… a guy on my bus. I don't know, and I don't know who stabbed him."

"Peter Gerrans did the stabbing," said Amy. "My mom texted me about it."

"Her mom's a nurse," Gina reminded me.

"Isn't that a privacy violation?" I asked.

"No," said Amy. "Because she didn't tell me who the victim was, and that's who's protected by HIPAA."

"Yeah," said Gina. "It's a perfectly legal smearing of his name by rumor. You try to lock people up for that and every small town in the US would be in prison."

"Girls," said Mr. Martinez, standing by our row for the third time.

Only now did I realize he was chuckling.

"We're talking about civil rights," said Gina.

"And healthcare policy," Amy added.

"And I'm… being a bad influence," I said.

"Please do it more quietly. You're making me look like I can't control my class."

"Just tell Principal Garcia that we're a bunch of hooligans," said Amy.

"Oh yeah, like that makes us stand out." Gina rolled her eyes.

"Don't make me send you to the office," he said. "If I have to sit through this, so do you."

"Do you know who got stabbed?" I asked.

"Yeah," said the girl who sat on the other side of Gina. "Who got stabbed?"

"I don't know," he said. "I didn't have time to find out before we got called to–"

"Mr. Martinez?" Principal Garcia blared.

I had completely forgotten that she was still talking, which was something else I had never done before.

"My students are concerned about another incident this morning," he hollered back. "It's all very upsetting."

He was telling the truth, but I also had the sense he was conspiring with us, legitimizing our whispering during an assembly while the other faculty glared.

"There's been a lot going on," the principal replied.

"Wait, what happened?" someone else in the stands below us shouted.

"There was an altercation on a bus."

"A stabbing!" someone else shouted. It was a female voice and might well have belonged to one of the girls at my bus stop. They'd seemed so quiet and withdrawn before.

"Who got stabbed?" called out another voice.

"I can't say right now," said the principal.

"Romy Valdez!" someone else shouted.

The name hit me like a slap in the face, even though I didn't know who she was. My inner sexist had assumed that the stabbing victim would be male.

Gina shut her eyes and shook her head.

"Who's she?" I asked. There was a rising hubbub all around us so I had to actually speak, rather than whisper.

"I don't know her well," she said, "but she's cute and Pete is kind of into harassing girls."

A sensation like chilled fingers wrapping around the base of my spine made me squirm. I didn't want to ride a bus where cute girls got stabbed by guys who couldn't take no for an answer.

"Can you take me to the DMV today?" I asked Gina.

"Huh?"

"The Department of Motor–"

"Oh, the MVD? Yeah. I thought you had to stay off the grid, though?"

"People get stabbed on my bus route."

"I can give you rides."

"No," I said. "I live way too far out."

"No, you don't. I don't want you shot or stabbed, okay?"

By now we were almost shouting because the din had risen and a few people were on their feet.

"I can't talk about the incident on the bus!" Principal Garcia shouted. "I'm sorry. We'll give you details when we have them."

A few rows down from us, two girls started shoving each other. I assumed it was all in good fun, until one of them stood up and slapped the other, hard enough to knock her over.

Everyone's attention swung towards the girl who fell down two levels on the bleacher and hit her head. People surged to their feet and even though I did too, my view was completely obstructed.

"Hey!" the principal's voice blared over the sound system, loud enough to hurt my ears. "Everyone sit down now!"

I obeyed, as did most of the rest of the school, but not everyone. Some students were crowding around the injured girl and throwing punches. I did not feel safe. The bleachers were packed and one person's fall could quickly cause a domino effect.

"What is going *on*?" Gina remarked as we were all pushed back by the chain reaction of someone being shoved several seats away.

I got to my feet so that I could get out of the way, just as the doors of the gym flew open and uniformed police officers poured in.

Well, okay, there weren't enough to *pour* in, but there were half a dozen, more than I'd seen in one place since I'd been in an actual police station. They didn't have their weapons drawn or anything, but one did have a bullhorn.

"Everyone stop what you're doing!" the officer hollered. "Freeze. All of you."

I put my hands up. I felt like I was in a movie about an American high school again, but not one of the fun ones. Was I about to become one of those statistics I'd looked up a few days ago?

But their attention was drawn by one of the larger fights. "Stop it now!" Mr. Bullhorn ordered as all the officers headed down to the lower left corner of the bleachers.

"Let's get out," Mr. Martinez ordered, gesturing at the back door.

I wondered if that was allowed. I had no idea what to do while police officers were trying to stop a fight. As the rest of the crowd surged toward the exit, though, I saw that Mr. Martinez had the right idea.

Gina, Amy, and I bolted for the door, piling through as the crowd came welling up behind us.

I lost my two friends soon after in the general chaos as people poured through the doorway in a stampede. Safety, I figured, was by the walls, but even there I got slammed into by other students, frantic to get away, so I just put my arms up to protect my head and cowered until the onslaught died down and the last of the stragglers emerged. The door slammed shut ominously behind them.

I lowered my arms and peered around. A couple of students were on the floor, gripping their legs where they'd been kicked or stepped on. Otherwise the hallway was empty, and now quiet enough that I could dimly hear the din of the police shouting inside the gym.

My stomach was clenched tight as a fist, and even this moment of calm didn't do anything to ease it. I started down the hallway towards the stairs, only to realize that I was shaking so hard that I nearly tripped over my own feet.

This was it, my limit for trauma for a single month. I'd endured a vampire drinking my blood, a supernatural transition, the murder of my father, my aunt's partial breakdown, and now this. The old adage that life never gave you more than you could handle? I was pretty sure that was a lie.

I pressed my palms to the cool cinder block wall. One of the students seated on the floor a few paces away was crying on her phone.

I took a couple of deep breaths, and then I got my phone out of my pocket and dialed Corban. Enough was enough.

It went straight to voicemail. "Hey," I said after the beep. "It's Liana. I know what you are, and you need to come back. Taos is falling apart without you."

15

Sunday morning hit like a welding torch, a giant one that could burn my whole body at once. I struggled to breathe as I felt my body begin to swell, like I was a giant blister that would pop at any second, showering the room with pus and blood.

If that sounds disturbing, it barely scratched the surface of the panic that erupted inside of me. I couldn't pray for help, as even my mind was only capable of wordless screams, but I knew I must be dying and hoped that my sacrifice would earn me some brownie points in the hereafter.

Relief, when it came, was like an explosion. My body gave out and the heat and pain ejected themselves in one last violent burst.

It was then that I realized my phone was ringing. I peered at the display and saw it was Corban.

Oh no. He probably thought I was an idiot or crazy or both. How was I going to explain my message to him? I hadn't expected him to listen to it, really. I'd been so wrapped up in my theories about him that I almost forgot he was a real person, and when he hadn't replied for two days, I'd been able to put him out of my mind.

I cleared my throat and recited the alphabet, half-hoping the call would go to voicemail before I was done. It didn't, so I answered. "Hi."

"Liana?"

"Yeah…"

"It's Corban. Sorry it took me so long to call you back. What's going on?"

I shut my eyes and bit my lip. What was I supposed to say? I felt like an idiot. "Um… sunrises are getting worse," I said.

"How so? More painful?"

"Much."

"But you're still able to walk around during the day?"

"Yeah, but I don't know for how much longer. This morning, I was sure I was a goner."

It was several seconds before he replied. "I'm sorry. As far as I've been able to learn, your condition isn't stable. Won't be stable. I'm amazed you're still you, to be honest. And very, very relieved."

"Is anyone here covering for you? Anyone who could deal with me if I turned?"

"I can't answer that. I'm sorry."

I sighed. "Sorry to call you."

"Why? I gave you my phone number for a reason. What else is happening around Taos?"

"Someone got stabbed on the bus Thursday. School was cancelled Friday. We've had fights and someone tried to burn down the library. And my aunt's been having a hard time."

"Your aunt has always had her ups and downs."

"I know."

"The rest of what you said, though? That's not great."

"Where did you go?" I asked.

"I went to figure out who turned you. Looks like the nest in New England is active again."

"That sounds bad."

"It is. Anyway… I'm trying to get back to Taos. I'll do my best, okay?"

Trying? I wondered. What was stopping him? "Okay… good luck."

"And I'm sorry I was gone for so long. That wasn't my plan." There was real regret in his voice.

My impulse was to say, "That's okay," but I wasn't sure that made sense. It wasn't as if he owed me anything. "Good luck getting home" was what I decided to say.

"Thanks. I'll find you once I do."

As we hung up I reminded myself that this did not mean he'd find me first thing when he got back. I had no idea what else was going on in his world, or even what his world entailed. I put my phone aside and shut my eyes, waiting for a different kind of agony to pass.

GINA CAME TO get me after breakfast, and brought me to church with her. It felt like a million years since the last time I'd been to church, and when I walked in, I felt like I was in a different century.

Not that the church looked run down or decrepit. Rather, it looked like a centuries-old Spanish mission, and might very well have been. The roof was held up with vigas, the stations of the cross were done in a bright, folk-art style, the priest wore simple-looking robes, and the service was nominally in English, but sprinkled liberally with Spanish. Only the carpet beneath my feet and the rest of the congregation was modern. Everyone wore nice skirts and slacks at best, and there were several of us in jeans (which Gina told me to wear for the tamale making later). We sat in the back, away from her parents and brother, who was an altar boy.

I expected to feel like I was intruding, but I didn't. There were a ton of students from the high school there, and none of them looked at me like I didn't belong. Me being an Anglo didn't seem to be much of an issue either, even though I was in the distinct minority. I got the impression, though, that church was just another part of everyday life for this population.

When we stepped outside, it was a bit of a shock to see a parking lot instead of a dusty road with burros carrying firewood. I'd been deeply immersed in the old West. Gina and I got into her car and went to grab lunch at a fast-food place.

Then it was time to head to Amy's. I tried not to fidget like a kid on a road trip as we drove on another road out of Taos that I'd never been on before. It branched off the main road that led to Cassie's subdivision. Rather than following that main road around to the left, we went right, and soon the houses and buildings gave way to open landscape.

It still boggled my mind how small and isolated Taos was. My boarding school campus had been remote, but it was unique because it was remote. Most towns in upstate New York had other small towns right up against them. Any space between towns was created by the giant parking lots of Super Walmarts and Home Depots. Here there wasn't enough of a customer base for a single Super Walmart.

There were also signs every half mile or so advertising the pueblo, and that was strange to me too. What must it be like to live somewhere that was also a tourist attraction? Did it feel like living in a human zoo?

But Gina turned off the road and onto a dirt track before we reached the place all those signs pointed to.

"Are we going into the pueblo a different way?" I asked, pointing to a sign that was fast diminishing in our rearview mirror.

"The signs are all pointing to, like, the main pueblo," she said. "But people don't usually live there year round. Every family owns a room in one of the great houses inside the wall, but inside the wall they can't have running water and electricity and stuff, so most people live outside the wall in regular houses.

People who live inside the wall, they tend to just do it in the summer."

"And if they never do, but they still own rooms?" I asked, my voice shaky because of how the car rattled and shimmied as we drove along. It looked like whoever had graded the road had been going too fast, causing their grading blade to skip and create a washboard effect.

"They'll set up shop there," said Gina. "Or just maintain them for heritage's sake, I guess. I dunno. Amy's gran sells dolls from their family's shop."

I felt like I was in another country, and at the same time realized I'd better not say that aloud. Amy's people were not the foreigners here.

A one-story house that looked much like those I'd seen all over town jounced into view. It had the same stucco-looking walls, except they weren't stucco. There were tufts of straw sticking out and one of the corners had crumbled to reveal mud bricks underneath. This was real adobe. Old adobe.

The house was also very rambling, as if it had started with one or two rooms and other rooms had been added from there, all on the same level.

We pulled up and Gina killed the engine, then proceeded to get out of the car and stride right through the back door of the house without knocking.

I jogged to stay on her heels, since I did not want to be seen barging in on my own.

We went from the blinding sunlight into a very dim mudroom, which had a scrap of linoleum laid on an uneven floor. I couldn't be sure, but I thought the floor underneath was dirt. The air was saturated with the smell of roasted chile and hot cornmeal.

Gina stepped up a step into the kitchen. I scrambled to follow, also stepping up from the uneven linoleum of the mud room to linoleum on a flat floor, likely a concrete slab.

I wondered if the house really had been built with a slab foundation only in the kitchen, because it sure looked like we had to step down again to go into the living room. The kitchen counters and cabinets were set square and level. A brand-new looking stove had three giant pots on it, lids rattling as their contents simmered. Near the stove was a dishwasher that had the ramshackle look of something that had broken down long ago.

"Hello, Gran!" Gina called from the far end of the kitchen as she stepped down into the living room beyond.

"Hello, hello," said an elderly woman seated on a dusty, woven-blanket-covered couch that came into view as I caught up to Gina.

Amy's gran was stacking cloth dolls with pretty velvet dresses in a cardboard tray that was probably the lid of a file box. Her hands were gnarled and wizened and her lips had the pulled-in look of someone missing a lot of teeth. Thus I wasn't surprised when she looked up and flashed a smile that was mostly gums.

"This is Gran," said Gina. "Everyone calls her Gran."

"I'm everyone's gran," Gran agreed.

That should not have choked me up, but it did. I didn't remember my grandparents. They'd all died by the time I'd turned four.

"This is Liana." Gina flipped her hand in my direction.

"Hello, hello," said Gran, though her gaze had returned to her dolls, which I was grateful for.

I wasn't in the mood to cry in front of a stranger, especially a stranger offering to be my gran.

Gina strode on and I stayed on her heels as we went down a half step through a room with a washer and dryer, clotheslines, and a door to the outside, then up a quarter step into a hallway. At the end of the hallway, on the right, was a bedroom, also with a dirt floor covered mostly in woven rugs.

Amy was sprawled out on a bed with an antique-looking brass frame and one of its feet propped up on a block of wood to keep it level. There was a metal desk, like what one would get from a military surplus store, against one wall, and in the corner there was a clothing rack on wheels, like what department stores used so that clerks could wheel clothes around to restock. This, apparently, was Amy's closet.

More tears welled up in my eyes, but I did not want to break down. Not now. Not here.

My friends were both staring at me, Amy still sprawled out, Gina seated on the edge of the bed.

"You okay?" Amy asked, getting up and coming over to hug me.

That did it. I started to cry. It was mortifying, but I couldn't stop. My shoulders were shaking and my eyes overflowed with tears.

"Augh, this week," said Gina. "Everything's been so hard this week. I don't know what it is. You sure you're okay, Liana?"

I managed to take one deep breath, then another. I pulled back from Amy before I could get her shirt wet from my tears. "I'm okay," I whispered. "I just miss my dad is all."

"Oh, yeah. You okay for a family thing here?" asked Gina. "Or you want me to take you home?"

I did want to go home, but not to the place I shared with Aunt Cassie. I wanted to go *home* home, to Southampton, to my room with its own balcony right above my dad's office, or to the Hawke Academy. Even though I had no real friends there, it was familiar and normal and part of a life I'd never, ever get back.

I put my hands over my face and forced myself to breathe as I shook my head. "Sorry," I whispered. "Just miss my old home."

"Well, yeah," said Amy. "I know a mud hut with dirt floors is not your idea of–"

"You have a nice house," I cut her off. "It looks like it's been in your family for a while." Besides, it made me think of all the New York state senators who claimed to be of the people. In New Mexico, this appeared to be an actual thing, legislators who lived normal lives fed by history, culture, and economic reality.

"Sure," said Amy, "and it's probably built on a site where my ancestors camped out and hunted deer." Her tone said that she thought this made her boring. I could not imagine having roots that went so deep in any one place.

I finished wiping my eyes. "How much of your family lives here?"

"Me, my mom, my gran, my brother for now. Sometimes my cousin stays with us. It's, you know, kinda chaotic."

That was more family than I'd ever had alive at one time, but I needed to not spend this visit sobbing and wallowing.

"Quick, distract her," said Gina. "Before she gets sad again."

Amy held up her phone with a picture of a guy sitting, slouched, on the arm of a couch, holding up a clay pot with a bear claw glyph on the side. "His name's Jack, and I finally emailed him, and he emailed ba-ack!" The sentence ended in sing-song.

"Did he make that pot?" I asked, realizing at once that this was the silliest question I could have asked. She was trying to share news of her crush, and here I was still boggled that he, too, was a teenage working artist.

But she smiled. "Yeah."

"Wow."

"And his dad is a *jeweler*, who would totally take Gina on–"

"I'm not commuting from here to Santa Clara to learn basic smithing," snapped Gina.

"But you'll waste your time–"

"Augh…" Gina flopped back on the bed and pulled a pillow over her face.

Amy gave me a long-suffering look and pointed to her bed, a clear invitation for me to sit.

I went and perched myself on the edge, but the mattress was so squishy I almost slid off. Amy shifted over so that I could lay on my side along the foot of the bed.

Gina pulled the pillow down to her chest and held out her hand for Amy's phone.

Amy handed it over, and Gina looked at the screen.

"I thought he did black," she said.

"Everyone does black pottery whenever they get soot on the clay while it's being fired. This is harder." Amy pointed at her phone screen.

"Oh, got it."

I clearly looked like I did not get it, because Amy rolled back towards me and held out the phone once more. "So, like, making a pot like this and keeping all the clay its natural color is hard. If it, I dunno the technical terms or anything, but if it gets black marks on it during firing, then you can fire it again so that it goes all black. It's pretty that way too, but this is harder."

I nodded. "So you're saying he's really good."

"Yeah… and probably gonna make real money during market season." She ducked her head slightly as she smiled at that.

"Amy!" shouted a voice down the hall. "We need help getting the tables set up."

"What?" she hollered back, glancing at her phone again. "We can't start on time, Mom!"

"And why not?"

"I've got guests. I'm teaching them about our culture. Starting on time isn't the Indian way."

"How 'bout I show them our attitudes about corporal punishment if you don't get out here?"

"Fine." She rolled her eyes. "Let's go."

"Do you use the word Indian?" I asked.

"Sometimes." Amy shrugged as she hopped off her bed.

I wished I could question her more, but I also didn't want to spend my first visit to my Native American friend's house asking her all the ins and outs of her Native Americanness. I suspected that living in a tourist attraction probably made her tired of answering these kinds of questions.

Besides, it was better to spend the day learning people's names, not their views on how their ethnic group was referenced.

I touched my cheeks gingerly, but they weren't even raw from my tears, so I hoped nobody else would know I'd cried.

We went out through the laundry room, into the blinding sunlight, and around into the shade of the house, where three guys were hoisting an old and decrepit picnic table so that it was end to end with another, much newer looking picnic table. All three guys looked about college age and had their hair buzzed short.

The ground here smelled slightly moist, as the house had shielded it from the worst sun of the day. The snow from a few days ago had long since melted, leaving bedraggled desert grass exposed to the air once more.

"That's my brother, Pedro," said Amy, pointing to the wiry guy on the far side of the tables. "Matt–" she pointed to the tall guy on the left, who was looking at a spot on his shirt with grim interest "–and that guy. We don't talk to him." She pointed to the stocky one on the right who was walking around the tables towards us.

"Some people don't talk to me," he said. "I'm Noah." He nodded in greeting and seemed nice. I wondered what Amy's issue was with him.

She gave him a rather cool nod in return.

Oh, I thought. Had they dated? Had she liked him and had her heart broken? Had he stood her up one night?

His lingering look to her was wistful, but another group of people came around the side of the house, with Gran in the lead, and their arrival broke apart the tension.

"Alright," Gran said with a clap of her hands. "I need the pots of filling on that end." She pointed to the far end of the new picnic table, the one that still had pale wood and no rust on the metal. "I need the cornhusks there." She pointed to the end of the old, gray, rusted picnic table, where it abutted the new one. "Now, now, now." She punctuated each repetition with a clap.

The three guys scattered while Amy sat down at the old picnic table.

"Liana, you sit there." Amy pointed to a seat on the far side of the new table. "Gran, Liana can do fillings, right?"

"Yes, yes. Now Regina, dear, I need you stacking and counting."

It took me a moment to realize this was Gina's full name.

More people were gathering and the guys came around the corner with two of the big pots, contents steaming. Pedro laid down a folded towel to protect the new wood and Noah and Matt waited to make sure there were enough people sitting down to counterbalance the tables before they set the pots down.

I went around to my place and stepped over the bench so I could sit. I was glad I was one of the first there; it was hard to climb into a picnic table bench when it was crowded. The wood creaked under my weight as I settled in.

Pedro ended up opposite me and he shot me a conspiratorial smile, as if he knew what it was like to be the new kid in the crew.

16

att set down a plastic washtub full of water and cornhusks in front of me and the guys at the end of the table finally put down the heavy pots. The whole table and bench tilted slightly under their weight.

"Okay," said Pedro, reaching into the tub between us on the table and taking out a cornhusk. "I'm going to cut the strips we use to tie the tamales. Liana, you want to take one cornhusk at a time and put filling in it?"

Noah handed me a plastic plate while Pedro pulled the tub over so that there was space for me to put it down on the table. Amy also got a plastic plate.

"Take one cornhusk," he said, "and lay it on the plate."

Someone, I didn't see who, set a bowl full of steaming corn mush next to me, and another bowl of what looked like a chile stew. The two smells together made my stomach rumble, even though lunch had been less than an hour ago.

More people were crowding around the table, ready for this whole production to begin.

I took a cornhusk and shook off the excess water, then set it down on the plate.

"So I usually take one spoonful of the cornmeal mix and spread it out on the cornhusk, and half a spoon of the chile in the middle." Pedro demonstrated

I did my best to follow his lead, then passed the cornhusk and filling to a woman who I assumed was Amy's mom, seated next to me. She had Amy's same smile and cocked her head the same way when she was concentrating.

Pedro handed her a little strip of cornhusk and she deftly folded the tamale shut and tied it off, then passed it to Gina, who put it in a casserole dish.

Amy began filling cornhusks like a machine and her mom was folding them even faster.

I had to up my game.

The water was slightly warm when I dipped a hand in, but the air was so dry and wicked the water off so fast that I found my fingers trembling slightly from the cold. This slowed me down, so I decided it was better to do it right than to do it fast. No matter how copious the fillings were, I didn't dare waste any.

"You guys using the oven or the horno?" asked an older man who came around the side of the house, walking stiffly as if his hips ached. His graying hair was pulled into a tight braid down the middle of his back.

"El horno!" said Amy, as if that alone was reason for a party.

Everyone else had their heads down, working. "What's an horno?" I asked Pedro.

"Outdoor oven," he said. "An old-fashioned kind that's made out of adobe."

"Oh."

"I'll show you once we're done here," said Amy. "It's kind of an adobe dome and you heat it up by burning a fire inside, then you pull out all the ash and it stays hot for hours. Long enough to do loaves of bread and a whole bunch of batches of tamales."

"So that's what you guys used before modern ovens?" I asked.

"Yeah…" said Pedro. "I think the Spaniards brought them, actually. I dunno what we used before."

"I think it was a technology called fire-in-an-open-pit," quipped Amy. "An ancient tradition among our people. Not sure I can explain it to you."

"I think my ancestors mainly used fire to burn down other people's villages so that they could steal all their stuff," I replied, before my brain could catch up with my mouth.

Everyone around me laughed at that, much, much harder than I would ever have expected.

"Is Linacre a Viking name?" Amy asked.

"No, English. But we went through our setting-other-people-on-fire phase too."

Now the whole table was laughing. "That's how civilized people do it, eh?" called out Matt.

More laughter.

I had no idea whether I ought to join in or not, but Amy caught my eye and gave me a wink, which was a relief. Apparently this joke I'd cracked was okay, even if I didn't fully understand how it was being taken.

Gina was stacking tamales and handing off the casserole dishes to Noah, who took each one and ran them around the side of the house.

The sun climbed in the sky and the shadow of the house slid until the end of the table with the fillings was exposed, causing the filling-doler-outers to have to shield their eyes, even with sunglasses on.

People came over in a steady stream, and I wondered if Amy's family had put the word out, or if this was a normal Sunday afternoon. People shouted greetings in English, Spanish, and another language that I later found out was Tiwa. I didn't know why it surprised me that Amy's people still spoke their indigenous language. In my old life, Native Americans were seen as this distant culture that had pretty much died out in the remote past. Today was a crash course in how wrong I was, as more and more people of all ages showed up, bringing their elderly relatives, their dogs, and their small children who toddled around, big brown eyes taking in the scene.

Someone brought a cooler full of soft drinks and ice and someone else brought a great big dispenser full of punch. Paper plates and plastic cups appeared as the tamale making wound down and people started to get up from the table.

By now the sun was halfway to the horizon and deep amber in color.

Amy stuck by my side and took me around to the horno. It was, like she had said, a dome-shaped adobe construct, though a very steep dome, kind of like a beehive hairdo. The air around it was saturated with the scent of wood ash. The oven came up to about chest height on me and had an opening in the base that was covered with a wooden panel. Near the top was a hole that was the chimney. There was black charring on the adobe around it.

While we stood there, Gran came around, put the wood panel to one side to reveal the opening, and reached in with a long paddle on a stick, like what pizzerias used to place pizzas in their wood-fired ovens.

And then it hit me that this was essentially the same technology.

Gran deftly removed three casserole dishes full of tamales and set them on wooden blocks beside the horno. Then she extracted two loaves of bread that she put on a towel draped over her arm, and put in three more casserole dishes (brought around the side of the house by Noah) before putting the wood panel back. Noah picked up one of the finished casserole dishes and Gran handed Amy and me hot pads to pick up the other two.

"Is it still hot?" Noah asked Gran, nodding towards the horno.

"Yeah, it's still good. Not hot enough for more bread, but the tamales will be fine."

I wondered how long Amy's ancestors had been making tamales just like this. The Spaniards, I knew from history class, had shown up in the mid-fifteen hundreds. Were tamales Spanish? Or were those indigenous? I'd been to Spain and eaten a lot of paella and seafood. A discreet search on my phone revealed that tamales were indeed indigenous, but had originated farther south, in modern day Mexico.

Gran limped off, back around the house.

"Your family's really nice," I said.

Amy smiled. "Yeah, they are. Usually. Sorry if this is all weirding you out?"

I shook my head. "I've just never had a family as big as yours. I don't even have any cousins."

She blinked in surprise, then quickly schooled her features. "They're not all that great," she joked. "If you want any of mine, let me know."

"How many do you have?"

"I'm not sure. Here in Taos I've got three, but my dad's Lakota, and I don't know what he'd call a cousin."

"What do you mean?"

"Like, some tribes will call anyone in the same clan a cousin, then you end up with a gazillion cousins. I don't even know if my dad's people do clans. There are so many different systems that Native groups use, it can get complicated."

Taos, I continued to realize, was utterly foreign and yet unequivocally American. The kind of place that showed exactly how broad and deep America could be.

"The thing is tha–" Before she finished the word, an old, beat-up pickup truck painted powder blue with panels of primer gray and splotches of rust came rolling towards the house from the road.

17

*A*my squared her shoulders, picked up one of the cooling casserole dishes, and marched back around to the picnic tables. I quickly grabbed the other one and followed her and we got there just as half a dozen guys in their twenties swaggered up carrying what looked like six packs of beer.

"Hey!" snapped Gran. "What's in those?"

"It's root beer, Gran," said Pedro.

"Is it actually root beer?" Amy stormed over, put down her casserole dish, grabbed a bottle, opened it by smacking the cap against the edge of the table, and took a whiff.

"They twist off," said another of the guys, demonstrating with another bottle, then taking a deep swig.

"It's root beer," Amy confirmed.

Pedro was greeting his friends with slaps on the back.

Gran was still scowling at them.

Gina sidled up to me. "Yeah…" she muttered. She pointed to a trivet on the table for me to set down my casserole dish, which I did, lifting it high enough so that I didn't burn any one scurrying around.

"What's wrong?" I asked Gina, once I'd settled it in place and stepped back.

"It would be just like them to bring beer."

"Aren't they over twenty-one?" They certainly looked it to me.

"This is reservation land. Alcohol is illegal."

"It is?"

She was watching Pedro draw his friends off to the side, her lips pinched. "Yep. Prohibition never got repealed here. Or… I don't actually know if that's how it worked, but no booze on a rez."

Pedro was talking to his friends, several of whom glanced in our direction. After a few moments, they nodded, exchanged slaps on the back again, and went back to their truck, Pedro with them.

As they climbed in (some back in the bed) and pulled away, raising a cloud of dust, Amy scowled. This whole tamale making party was for Pedro, and he'd just taken off.

There was a moment of awkward silence, and then Gran resumed serving tamales and everyone fell back into the rhythm of talking and laughing, though Amy stayed silent as she drew me over to the table to get my own plate and tamales.

"These are the less spicy ones," she said.

They were amazing. My first forkful brought an explosion of taste across my tongue. There was the hearty grit of the cornmeal, the sharp bite of the chile, and the meaty richness of the pork all mixed together.

I chased it with a mouthful of punch and shut my eyes, savoring it all.

The picnic benches were soon all occupied by the older set, several of whom walked with canes and walkers, and the youngest children who piled onto their laps. Amy and I went over to where Gina stood and ate our meal there.

"Yeah, so you think they're all right?" Gina quipped, nodding at my plate of rapidly disappearing tamales.

"Yeah," I said. "So good."

"I'm not sure if it's the horno, or just all the work that goes into them," she said. "I mean, things taste better when you have to expend effort, you know?"

"I wouldn't know, actually." I wondered if the view wasn't a factor, though. From where we stood we took in an expansive vista of the valley with a few other houses with metal roofs in the middle distance. The sky arched high overhead, wisps of cloud-like daubs of paint in an oil painting, and the sun was starting to set the horizon on fire.

"Like when you hike up into the mountains and make Cup O'Soup?" said Gina. "Tastes amazing even though it's the same stuff."

"I've never carried my own food on a hike," I confessed. "Call me sheltered."

But Gina only shrugged.

Amy wasn't paying attention to us, but rather frowning after her brother and the small cloud of dust generated by that powder-blue truck, speeding off into the distance.

"He'll be fine," Gina said to her.

"I hate those guys." Amy stabbed at her tamale. "Bunch of creeps."

WE STAYED UNTIL the sun set and the first stars appeared in the royal-blue sky above. I couldn't stop staring at the gorgeous tones the heavens took on as the sun said farewell. It almost eased my nervousness about being out after dark. Almost.

I'd managed the bus trip from New York with its overnight legs and survived every sunrise, but back then I didn't know what kind of fire I was playing with.

The uneaten tamales were packed into disposable tupperwares and I was given one, something I worked hard not to cry over, it was such a kindness.

Gina and I piled into her compact car and soon we were bumping our way back to the main road.

"Thanks for the ride," I said.

"Yeah, of course. I'm glad you could come."

"Me too."

"Pretty different from New York?"

"You could say that." I laughed and she joined in.

The crystal hanging from her rearview mirror clacked against the windshield as we turned onto the paved road, where Gina was able to speed up.

The sky was growing darker and the stars were getting brighter and more numerous. I angled my gaze as far upward as I could through the closed car window and wondered if I'd be able to sleep tonight. On one hand, I was spent. On the other, I wasn't sleepy. If I had another wakeful night, I'd at least have some new happy memories to keep me company. I'd felt family around me again, even if it wasn't my family.

"I need to fill up," said Gina.

The dark amber lights of a gas station were visible in the near distance. "Do you want me to pay?" I asked.

"What? No." She snorted.

I figured pushing it might only insult her. The car glided from the darkness into the harsh lights over the fuel bays and she guided it to a pump. When she got out, I figured I would, too. If she wouldn't let me pay, maybe I could wash the windows or something.

She put the nozzle in the gas tank, started it pumping, then said, "I need to use the bathroom."

I watched her stride away towards the bluish, fluorescent lights of the attached convenience store.

The temperature was cold, of course, but I found it rather pleasant. I went to get the squeegee for the windows and found that it was missing. I peered over at the next set of pumps over, squinting in the dimness to see if the squeegee for that one was there.

A group of guys came out of the convenience store, laughing and shoving each other in a way that was meant to seem like good fun, but looked rather a lot like a show of dominance.

One of them stopped and looked at me.

Pedro stepped out behind them. "Hey, Liana!" he called out.

I waved.

"Liana, is it?" said the guy who'd been staring at me.

I couldn't make out much about him other than his silhouette. He was tall and muscular and had longish hair. He wasn't just looking at me, though. He was leering.

My blood should have run cold. I should have worried about my safety. But that wasn't what happened. Instead all my sleepless nights caught up with me and I felt my body begin to change. I could smell the scent of these guys' warmth in the rapidly cooling night. My stomach growled with a new kind of hunger I'd never felt before.

18

ll of the guys turned their attention to me, now, looking like baggy silhouettes thanks to their loose jackets and sagged pants.

I held as still as possible, fear clawing its way up my spine. White fire arced through my heart. I no longer saw the silhouetted figures, only sensed their warmth. Even from this distance, I could detect their pulses, my gaze narrowed in on the throat of the nearest one, where the jugular throbbed rhythmically. Saliva flooded my mouth and I shut my eyes.

"Hey, leave her alone," I heard Pedro say. "That's my sister's friend."

"Why you just standing out here alone?" another of them called out.

I could get back in the car, I reasoned. Maybe with its sturdy door between me and them, I'd be able to break off this bloodlust I felt.

But I couldn't be sure. The guys continued to stare at me, silence stretching between us. I probably looked like I was terrified, the way I stood frozen. *Go get in the car,* I ordered myself, but my traitorous feet wouldn't obey.

One of the guys took a step closer, and I could all but feel my canines lengthening. I knew exactly how far I'd have to jump to sink my teeth into the artery in his neck and gulp down the gushing stream of blood. I didn't just want to feed on him. I wanted to drain him dry.

"Hey…" He was coming towards me now. One flimsy car door wasn't enough to put between us.

I slipped around the pump and into the darkness beyond, hoping that would put him off.

"Leave her alone," I heard Pedro shout. "Just, stop."

"Where's she going?"

"Hey, you gonna be okay?" chorused other voices.

They were still coming in my direction, I could feel it. I could smell them.

My choice was simple: I could end my mortal life as a vampire, killing those innocent guys. Or I could end my life on the run, hoping that if I put enough distance between myself and them, that I could spare their lives. I had no idea who else I might run into and kill once I lost my soul, but if it was a choice between knowing that I'd kill Pedro and his friends, and running off into oblivion, the choice was clear.

I stumbled in the dark. The world spun and ice cold asphalt smacked against my palms.

"Hey, you fell in the road," called out one of the voices.

So I had. I'd stumbled over the curb and fallen into the street. If it had been a busy street, I might have ended my misery that way, but it was Taos after dark. Totally dead.

I scrambled back to my feet and took off at a run, eating ground way faster than I ever had as a human. The crisp nighttime air was cooling still more, making the smell of warm bodies easier to pick up.

Or was it? Were the guys still behind me? Had they chased me? Were they the closest humans? Apparently vampires got scrambled by fear the way humans did.

I kept running anyway, even though I knew I was burning in my transition from human to vampire. I would be too far gone to survive sunrise, but maybe if I ran far enough, I could save all of Taos. Maybe I could go deep into the desert where there was no shelter from the sun, and there I could die a noble death.

"Liana!" shouted a distant voice behind me.

Gina. She probably thought I'd lost my mind, and perhaps that was for the best. It wasn't like I could double back and explain myself, and even if I could, what was I going to say, the truth? I'd probably bite and kill her before I got a word out.

The night around me was getting lighter, and not from an increased number of street lights. The darkness of night itself was going away. Looking up, I could still see the moon and stars clearly, but looking around, I could also see the sidewalk in detail, including the jagged crack that I was able to jump (rather than trip) over.

The scent of warm flesh was getting more potent, and a quick glance around revealed that of all the directions I could have run that would have taken me away from civilization, I'd chosen one that took me deeper in. Stupidly, I'd followed the road without thinking about what roads were for and who built them. Roads led to people; that was the main purpose of their existence.

Now I was nearing downtown, and I slowed my steps, the scent of warm-blooded humans overwhelming me. In the crush of adobe buildings crowding along the narrow alleys, I could tell where there were people still up working, or starting a night of drinking at a bar two streets over. I could smell and hear two men headed across the Plaza, which was probably four blocks away.

My mouth was watering so much that it was only a matter of time before I started drooling. The urge to chase down a person and dig my fangs into the soft flesh of their neck was like nothing I'd ever felt before. Perhaps if I'd ever done drugs or developed any addictions, I might have a reference point. As it was, it was merely a raw need, punching at the inside of my chest, ordering me to obey or suffer despair.

A force like a strong current pulled me towards the distant sound of a man's laugh. I fought against it and cast about for a direction to run that would give me freedom, but there were none. This tiny smattering of dwellings that barely even qualified as a city had me trapped.

I stopped walking. There was one direction that smelled clean, devoid of humans. In order to head that way, I had to scale a low adobe wall, which I was able to do much too easily, and drop down into a space that was an alleyway with its mouth blocked by a giant dumpster.

The dumpster looked black in the darkness, and its painted metal sheen was unmistakeable. At the sight of this obstacle, my resolve collapsed and I dropped to my knees, not caring how hard they slammed into the icy, packed snow.

I wanted to cry. I wished I could cry, but my eyes weren't burning with tears. Was I already dead? Had my body converted into a corpse and my soul departed? I still felt like me, but was I in fact a demon with Liana Linacre's memories? Was my disgust with myself contained in those memories?

Someone else dropped into the alleyway beside me, and I scrambled to get away, moving on my hands and knees until a wall made me stop.

"Liana?" The figure was tall, with broad, muscular shoulders and wavy blond hair.

Corban.

Was he back or was I hallucinating him? He didn't smell like a human, but he also didn't smell like cold stone. I couldn't pick up any scent, other than the tanned leather of his jacket and the slightly citrus scent of shampoo or body wash. The sight of him unleashed a panic in my chest and it was all I could do to stay where I knelt, cold air sawing across the skin of my throat as I pumped it in and out of my lungs.

Corban stood several paces away with his gloved hands out. "It's okay. Don't move, all right? You're still breathing. Let me help you."

Help me? Or kill me? Regardless of which it was, I knew I needed to stay put. He'd protect Taos because it was his job. He turned his head so that the moonlight fell across his face. His skin was unaffected by the cold. No reddened nose, no flushed cheeks, just his usual flawless complexion.

I turned so that my back was braced against the wall, my knees pulled up to my chest.

Corban circled to one side of me, no doubt hoping to avoid a hard kick once he was in range.

I hugged my knees to my chest and focused on keeping myself contained. Yes, he was a predator, but so was I. Corban said I was smart, so we might only get one chance for him to kill me before I learned his tricks and became more devious prey.

He stepped up to about two paces away on my left and kept his hands outstretched as he knelt down beside me. "You're okay," he said. "You haven't turned all the way. Just hold still, all right?"

"How long have you been following me?" I asked.

"I just got back into town."

"You shouldn't have left."

He ignored that and instead pulled off his gloves and tucked them in the pocket of his jacket. His breath didn't steam in the air, and his eyes stayed fixed on mine. Then he shut them, flexed his hands, and repeated, "Hold still, all right?"

I hugged my knees even tighter as he sidled around, so that he was in front of me, and put his hands over mine, pressing skin to skin.

Searing pain like sunshine shot through my arms and I shut my eyes tight as it spread through my chest.

Hold on, I told myself. *Hold on, hold on.* The pain was building, much like it had this morning, and now came the feeling that my whole body was swelling up like a great blister, ready to burst.

Corban gasped and his hands both spasmed as he held on, the skin of his palms feeling white hot against the backs of my hands.

More pressure built in me. I wondered how intense it would get and whether I would explode in flames or dust, like I'd seen on television. My panic levels should have been rising too, but the pain was a familiar friend at this point and I was at peace. I'd done what I could, had killed no one, and would leave the world no worse off than I'd found it. It was the best someone with my affliction could hope for.

Corban's breathing became labored and he leaned in as his fingers fought to open.

Tears burst from my eyes and spilled down my cheeks, taking all the pressure with them. The pain winked out and the world cleared.

Silence descended.

It was done.

And… I was still here. I felt the cold snow under me and the adobe wall behind me, the frigid air against my cheeks and in my lungs.

I'd survived? I could stay on planet Earth another day? Corban had let go of my hands, but he still leaned against my knees, bracing with his forearm.

I moved sideways along the wall, away from him, and he fell forward onto his hands, his hair tumbling over his face as he heaved deep breaths.

I sat up straighter and could hear the sound of blood rushing in my ears. My breath was steaming in the cool night air.

Corban pushed himself back to sit down hard in the dirt, his face still contorted in pain. "You okay?" he managed to gasp.

I looked down at myself and checked my pulse once more with my fingers against my throat. "Yeah."

"Good." He nodded.

"So it's true," I said. "You're an angel."

He looked over at me, gaze telling me what words couldn't. He regretted that I'd discovered his secret, but he was relieved, too.

19

"R U OK?" Gina's text popped up on my phone.

Corban glanced at my screen, leaning in close enough that if he were human, I'd be able to feel his body warm the air slightly, but he wasn't human. He was other, and even if he was a good kind of other, evidence of his otherness was creepy. "Gina's calm," he said. "And no, she didn't kill Pedro and his friends, or even yell at them too much."

I shot him a look of semi-confusion as I typed out the text, "Met up with Corban. He's driving me home." Because he was, whether he'd planned to or not. We had some talking to do.

"OK, cool, cool," was the reply.

"Are you an angel or a pot dealer?" I demanded. "What did you do to her?"

He chuckled at that, as if it was some incredibly novel joke. "I don't know if I can explain." He moved so that he could slump against the wall next to me, looking as if he'd had all the energy sucked out of him. Perhaps he had.

I expected his hands to be burnt, but when he turned his palms up to look at them, the skin was unblemished.

"But–" I began.

"Look, right now I'm really weak, and really starved, and you probably have all this fear and grief. Please, let me feed?"

Feed? "On my fear?"

He nodded, his face looking extra pale in the moonlight. "Yeah."

"But not my grief," I said. "No touching that." This was not the kind of conversation I thought I'd be having on a Sunday night, or any night for that matter.

"Fine. Just let me in."

"To my mind?"

"Yes, I'm not a mind reader. I just feed."

I had no idea how to let something like him into my mind, but I took a deep breath and told myself it was okay to let go of my fear of turning into a vampire. I'd generate enough to replace whatever Corban took by tomorrow night.

Sure enough, the creeping dread that loomed over me at all times bled away. My memories of nightmares about waking up in flames took on a paler, less ominous cast. The feeling like I had a cancer eating at my insides dissipated. I was just plain old Liana with some supernatural beauty slapped on over my plain old insides, and the knife-sharp grief that tore at my heart was still there, untouched.

"This," I said, "is bizarre. So you took away all of Gina's anxiety at her friend running off into the night?"

"I feed on emotions, negative ones." The color was returning to his cheeks and he pulled his gloves back on.

"Feeding doesn't sound very angelic."

"Fine, I absorb emotions. I unburden mortals from their pain. That better?" His eyes sparkled in amusement.

It was too weird of a situation for me to joke about, though. I tucked my hands into my pockets to keep them warm, though my core was losing heat while I sat on the frozen ground, and now that my body temperature was rising again, I was going to start melting whatever snow was under me. "So you *can* also read minds," I said. "Maybe not the actual thoughts, but you know whether or not someone's being made sad, or embarrassed."

"Hey, I'm not any better at figuring out why people feel how they do than a perceptive human, and the older I get, the harder it is for me to remember what makes people tick. In your case, you've shut me out since that first moment we met. Humans have the final say in what my kind can and can't do to them. That's the deal, right? Between humanity and divinity? Divinity is here if you'll let it in, but it's up to you to accept it."

"You fed off me before I let you in," I pointed out. "When we first met."

"Sometimes I get a taste before the blocking reflex kicks in, but when someone doesn't trust me, the reflex is natural. Everyone has it. Unless someone is willing to let go of their pain, or is so consumed by it that they can't function, I'm locked out. What makes you a little different is that you were aware of what was happening when your walls went up. People usually aren't."

"So you can't feed on my grief right now?"

"No." He shook his head, eyes shut as if his head ached. "And I wouldn't if I could."

My heart wanted to take pity on him, but my mind still had a lot to process. "What about creating a situation where humans can't get by without you? The high school fell apart when you left."

"You already knew that life is too hard to get through alone. People need to rely on the divine, however they define it, to endure the hardest parts. But if you're trying to make me feel guilty for shirking my duty..." He pushed his hair back from his forehead. "It's working. Though I should also point out that I'm not the only force for good in the world, or even in Taos. People always have access to divinity in more ways than one." He sounded so defensive that I finally let myself take pity on him.

"No... sorry." I leaned my head against the adobe wall behind me. "You left the ninety and nine to look out for me, and I'm sorry you had to."

"It's my job. And I found Evan and his sire."

"Oh yeah?" He'd met Evan? I purposely didn't dwell on that thought. "I never met his sire," I said.

"Her name's Darissa." He stood, stiffly and held out a gloved hand for me.

I took it and let his strong grip haul me to my feet. My cheeks flushed, even though I knew that was silly. Holding hands for the purpose of helping me up wasn't him flirting with me. He was being chivalrous. Nothing more.

My knees were stiff because of the cold, and the night was quiet, save for our hushed conversation. "You went all the way to New York?" I asked.

He shook his head. "No, I went to Albuquerque to fly out to New York, and I ran into Evan and Darissa instead. I got them on the run and drove them way out into the desert, but that'll only slow them down, not stop them. They know where to look for you because they broke into your father's office and went through his desk until they found a card from your aunt. They're determined to find you, and you know what it means when the two of them come after you together?"

"No... Wait a minute, my dad's office?"

"Yeah. Not the one in your house, the one where he worked."

"Darissa... did she kill my dad?"

Corban's expression was pure sympathy. "Yeah."

He said this as if he expected me to know already, as if it should have been obvious that his death was my fault, completely. By letting myself get wrapped up with Evan, I'd put my dad in the line of fire.

Those evenings making out with Evan burned in my gut now, causing bile to rise in my throat. What kind of idiot was I?

"Liana..." Corb frowned. "They're coming to kill you. One other thing vamps do that is convenient for controlling their numbers? They don't tolerate love rivals. Evan broke the rules when he turned you. Darissa's not going to forgive him until he kills you."

I did not care if I died for this. There was something else that upset me far more. The last family member I had left was in danger because of me. "If they follow me to my aunt's house, they're going to kill Cassie."

"Liana…" He put a gloved hand on my shoulder and looked me straight in the eye with an intensity that caused me to quake inside. "Before you feel all guilty, let me remind you that they would come here and eliminate her whether you were here or not. You being here gives your aunt a fighting chance."

My guilt was settling into my grief, making it sharper. I'd thought hearing that he'd died was the worst feeling possible. How wrong I was. There were a lot of depths below that one that I was sinking into now. My dad dying was life changing, but this was life ending. How could I keep going, knowing I'd made such a huge mistake?

Corban placed his hands on my shoulders and looked me in the eye. My guilt began to drain away, and at first I fought it, but his gaze was firm. "You were taken advantage of. You were out of your depth. The price you paid for your mistakes was unfairly high. I'm telling you the truth."

I took a deep breath, realized what he was doing, and pulled away, shutting him out. He'd already made his mark, though. I was intellectually aware of my guilt, but the raw emotion wasn't there. I expected *that* to make me feel guilty, but it didn't. It was like Corban had reset part of me, switching off the font of pain and instead clearing the space for rational thought. I swiped my cheeks with my hand once more and glared at him.

"It was overwhelming you," he said. "And that's a waste of time and spirit. You can't atone, Liana. Only one person in history could do that. If you try it, it's just wallowing." His blue eyes were unrepentant.

And I wanted to be angry with him, but I couldn't be. Some irrational annoyance surfaced up, but in my heart, I knew he was right. There was no point to feeling that much pain without any way of controlling it. Not feeling that much pain felt like a betrayal, though.

Killing Darissa would make up for that.

"What am I supposed to tell Cassie?" I asked. "I mean, we've talked about whether the vampire thing is a delusion or–"

"Wait, you told her about the vampire thing?" His eyes widened and his pupils began to dilate.

"Of course I did. I'm not gonna live in her house with this huge secret."

"Yeah but… no… never mind. Fine. You did that. Sounds good."

I didn't know how to reply to that, so I just stood there, blinking at him. The tear-tracks on my cheeks let the cold cut into my flesh like knives.

"You're unique," he said. "Honesty seems to be a part of how you fight the vampirism, so if you did that and you're still here with a beating heart and a reflection, then it must've been the right thing to do."

I wiped my cheeks with my bare hands. "But you think her life is hard enough with her OCD, so she doesn't need weird stuff like me talking about vampires."

His smile was wry. "She told you about that, did she? You're one of the privileged few. I don't know if your situation makes hers worse. I don't feed off Cassie so there's a lot I don't know about her. She handles herself well enough, and like I said, the older I get, the less I understand people."

I pushed my hands into my pockets and looked away. At least he was offering me some distraction. "How old are you?"

"Yeah…" He sighed. "This needs to be part of a longer conversation."

"Fine. You've got forty minutes before I need to be home and in bed."

"No, first we've got to talk about Evan and Darissa."

But I shook my head. Now that my thoughts were clear, I needed to be systematic and thorough. "I'm not talking about anything else with you until I understand what you are. Then, yes, you are going to tell me how to defeat them."

He shut his eyes and for a moment swayed on his feet. "Okay," he said. "Fine. But I'm still hungry so we're going to go to a burger place I know that is near an apartment block."

I wasn't sure why he asserted this so forcefully. Did he expect me to argue with him? Demand a burger place away from people, where he'd faint and be useless? Or maybe he thought I'd demand tacos instead? I was still full from all the tamales I'd eaten. I shrugged and looked at the wall I'd leapt over while still vamped out. "I need a boost, I think. Unless you have some cool, magical way of teleporting?"

He shook his head and laced his fingers together so that I could use his interlocked hands as a step. I managed to gain the top of the wall on the first try and throw a leg over. "How are you going to get out?" I asked. "Are you sure you can't teleport? I'm pretty sure I've seen you do it."

"I'm gonna walk." He pointed to the far end of the alley. "The dumpster doesn't completely block it off."

"Okay, so you just boosted me up onto this wall to make me feel ridiculous?"

He shrugged. "I dunno. You said it was what you wanted. I'll see you in a sec." He walked to the end of the alley, sidled past the dumpster, and was gone.

I waited for him to appear in the parking lot on the other side. "So do you have to do whatever I ask?" I asked.

"No, look… my head hurts. Don't ask me to think two moves ahead, or even one move ahead. If you could drive us to the burger place, that would be great."

"I can't drive."

"I'm sure you can figure out how." He pulled out his keys and his RAV4, which I now saw was parked a few feet away, lit up with a chirp.

"I don't have a license."

"It's New Mexico. They don't enforce stuff like that here."

I couldn't tell if he was being funny or not.

"I'm law abiding," I said. "I'm a rules girl."

"And I'm about to keel over from starvation, so please make an exception so that I don't die."

I studied him. Was he really on the brink of death? He did look pale, but beyond that, he looked tapped out, like he'd pulled multiple all-nighters on a required project that he just didn't care about anymore. It was pointless to keep arguing with him. "Does your car have gears?"

"Of course it has gears, but you don't have to shift them, if that's what you mean. It's an automatic."

I hopped down from the top of the wall, my boots hitting the icy asphalt with a thud, and held out my hand. "Fine."

"Thank you." He tossed me the keys.

I didn't even try to catch them. After all the effort he'd put forth into burning the vampirism out of me, I wasn't going to invite it back by trying to have reflexes. Human Liana did not have the eye-hand coordination to catch a beach ball. Keys were entirely out of the question, so I let them fall with a crash at my feet, then I stooped to pick them up.

Driving didn't seem too difficult in theory, and there wasn't any black ice on the road that I could see. "All right," I said. "Here goes nothing."

20

We pulled up to the burger joint a few minutes later, still in one piece with an undamaged car. I'd managed to keep between the lines the entire way, though the fact that there was no other traffic on the road lowered my odds of an accident considerably.

I still felt a gaping hole where guilt ought to have been. No matter how many times I reminded myself that it was my fault my father had died, my heart reacted as if it'd had years to think it over and make peace with the fact.

Yes, it was my fault, but dwelling on it did no good. If I wanted to do something about that, I needed to keep a clear head and find a way to end Evan and this Darissa chick.

Through the window, the place looked empty, save for a bored cashier leaning on the counter, staring wistfully into the distance.

"Are you going to eat actual food?" I asked Corban as I did my best to park. "Or do I have to eat food to pay rent on a table?"

After reversing twice, I decided I was more or less in the parking space and shut the car off.

"I'll eat," he replied, getting stiffly out of the car and stumbling up to the door of the restaurant.

I clambered out of the driver's seat and went to help him, pausing to lock the car by hitting the button on the key fob. Then I put the keys back in his pocket before considering how that would look. It made us look like a couple, and him leaning on me as we pushed through the doors only compounded the image.

But would anyone who saw us notice or care? Could Corban drain off curiosity much like he had my fear? Was curiosity a negative emotion?

And did he know how awkward I felt about having him lean on me? He said I could block him by wanting to, and I definitely wanted to. Even through the thick layers of my jacket and his, I was painfully aware of his well-muscled torso pressed to my side and his arm around my shoulders.

At the counter he ordered a burger, fries, and soda while I just settled for a hot chocolate, not because I needed the calories, but because I felt bad about using their space without paying at least a token amount. A few minutes later we were seated at a booth with our orders spread out between us, and I stared at him much like a scientist might stare at a lab rat as he took a bite of his burger. He'd taken off his gloves and stuffed them back in his pocket.

He looked back at me with a lifted eyebrow.

"So do you need food?" I asked. "Or are you just capable of eating it?"

"If I'm this drained, food helps," he said. "It takes the edge off the starvation and makes it easier to feed on emotions. Otherwise, no, I don't need it."

"Weird. So your metabolism somehow converts psychic energy into physical energy?"

"I don't know," he said, shooting me a look between bites that blended irritation with amusement. "If you want to talk nerdy, then fine, but if you want me to be able to understand you, dumb it down a bit, okay?" He wiped his mouth on a napkin as he chewed a mouthful of food.

The lights in the burger joint were bright enough that the window next to us was a solid field of darkness. If I looked hard enough past our reflections, I could see a few glints on Corban's car.

It was a relief to see my reflection. Corban's also looked perfectly human.

"So," he said. "How'd you figure it out?"

"That you're an angel?"

"Mmm-hmm."

I pulled my wallet out of my jacket pocket and produced the page from my journal.

He raised an eyebrow again as I unfolded it.

"So, first off," I said, "I figured vampires had to have a predator, or else they would have taken over the world."

"Sure."

"And I figured it wasn't some secret order of humans, because keeping it a secret seems like a pain and I don't get the advantage. If there's a public health threat like vampirism, just fight it publicly and air commercials and put up billboards. You guys have study data on vamps, so publish it. I figured if the predator was secret, there had to be a reason for it, like that predator not wanting to be known to humankind. Not openly."

He sipped his soda and nodded.

"You have the power to go invisible and maybe teleport," I said. "You poofed when you were in the bathroom with me, and in the grocery store, Amy couldn't see you."

"I can't teleport," he said. "And it's not really invisibility. It's the ability to be overlooked. You're not so bad at it yourself."

"What? Being mousy is a superpower? You're not mousy."

"Neither are you." He was clearly very amused that I'd called myself that, but when I scowled at him, he shrugged and said, "Fine, yeah, mine's a supernatural ability. I can make people not notice I'm around, or… most people. Sometimes I find one who can see me anyway." He gave me a pointed look.

"That why I kept seeing you around the school on Monday, when you didn't want me to?"

"Yes," he said. "And vampires can't ever see my kind. Not unless we're right in their face, messing with them or talking to them. You looking at me last Monday? That was a first for me."

"But some humans can always see you?" I asked. "Why?"

"Some humans have a knack for seeing things as they are."

"What?" I asked. "Like artists and–"

"I don't think that kind of art would sell. No. People who are hard to fool, who always think about what they're told, who examine a situation without prejudice, who don't take things at face value. They don't tend to be in one career over another. You find them in all kinds of random places."

I let that sink in, then looked at my list again. "You make jokes about really old movies."

"Old movies?"

"*All About Steve?* That movie where Sandra Bullock writes a guy's license number on her arm? That came out a decade ago. People my age don't quote a whole lot of movies from ten years ago, especially not ones that went nowhere at the box office and aren't classics in any way."

"You insulting my taste in movies?" he asked. "I thought it was hilarious."

"I guess I am."

He shrugged good-naturedly, and ate more of his burger.

I flipped my page of notes over. "You asked if I was religious," I said. "That seemed a little strange. People don't tend to ask that kind of thing these days. Your name: Corban means 'a sacrifice dedicated to God' and Alexander means 'warrior.' Seemed kinda on the nose."

Now Corban was laughing, though. "Whatever you say, Daughter of the Sun."

I blinked at him.

"That's your name."

"Oh."

"Sun, like the sun." He pointed upward. "You say my name's on the nose?"

"When my mom named me, I wasn't… never mind."

"Sorry," he said. "I digress. Continue." He nodded at my sheet of paper.

I looked down at it and collected my thoughts again. "The school fell apart once you left. People couldn't deal with their problems and they started fighting and tried to burn down the library. Nobody in school seemed to know much about you, or care. I mean, that's not normal. The mysterious hot guy that is nice to everyone? Girls usually have all kinds of details on him."

His wry smile made me realize I'd called him hot.

My cheeks grew warm and I looked back at my list. "Some people think you might be a narc, though."

"I know. The principal is one of them."

"The ritual you did in my room looked like a prayer and you said religious symbols work on vampires. You call vampires demons. Where there are demons..." I put my sheet of paper down. "There are probably angels."

"They do pretty much come from the same mythologies," he agreed.

"So you want me to burn this piece of paper? Or eat it? Or–"

"I think tearing it up will work just fine." He smirked at me as he held out the bag his burger had come in.

I tore the sheet of paper into tiny pieces and tossed them in.

"So," he said, "fine. What else do you want to know?"

This was my chance to ask him anything, and my mind was unhelpfully blank. I turned my gaze away from his handsome face to collect my thoughts.

"Okay," I said. "First of all, how much are you allowed to tell me?"

He swallowed, took a drink from his soda, then cleared his throat and nudged his fries towards me. "Hard to say. You're kind of a unique case. We do reveal ourselves to humans sometimes, but usually in situations where we know the person won't betray us."

"So… you think I might? Betray you?" I found him impossible to read. He wasn't looking at me with a suspicious glare.

He ate some fries, then said. "If you decide I'm up to no good? Yes. I think you would turn against me because you regret not turning against Evan."

I had to take care not to squeeze my cup of hot chocolate. A fountain dousing my face and clothes would not be a good look for me. "Why would you be up to no good? Aren't you guys supposed to be infallible?"

Corban was squirting ketchup out of a little packet onto a napkin, but he paused to look up at me. "No. We make mistakes. We can become evil. Like Lucifer and all that." He drank more soda and nudged his fries towards me again.

This time I gave in and ate some, wondering why he'd be pushing these starchy, salty death-sticks at a human being, with a beating heart and arteries that could clog. "So why should I trust you at all, then? You took away the guilt I should be feeling about my dad's death, based on what you think is right?"

"It was overwhelming you," he retorted, "and you still feel plenty guilty. You're just in a position that you can do something about it, instead of hurting so bad that you can't think straight."

The logic held, but it felt like a betrayal of my humanity to embrace it. Still, there was nothing I could do about it now. "Why are you talking to me at all then?" I asked. "If me turning against you is a risk?"

"Because you're interesting, and everything I've seen shows you have good judgment. If you decide I'm up to no good, there's a more than slight chance that you're right. You know, with your whole ability to fight vampirism and keep a demon from taking your body thing?" He winked.

I looked away. "I still got bitten."

"So you're not infallible either." He shrugged. "Actually, that's been the hardest thing, ever since I ascended. Seeing people get turned, because more often than not, they fell in love. My order believes that succumbing to a demon damns the soul, and that never seemed fair to me. Or cases like you where it was forced on you–"

"Turning wasn't forced on me," I said. "I agreed to that."

"After a guy had already worn you down and worked you over. No, you're evidence that maybe it's still possible for life to be fair. Maybe one monumentally bad decision doesn't have to be the end of the line for your immortal soul in every case."

Corban kept his gaze on me, as if watching to make sure that he hadn't hurt my feelings.

It was time to change the subject. "How did you… what was the word? Ascend?" I asked.

He cleared his throat again. "Well, I was sentenced to die–"

"So you were human?"

He nodded. "Yeah, I was born human. Lived to be about nineteen or twenty… I'm not sure. Somewhere around there. I broke a law about contributing to a public sacrifice because I was Christian and didn't want to support another faith. While I was in my cell, ready to be executed, a member of the order showed up instead and offered to elevate me."

"How?" I took a sip of my hot chocolate, feeling the granules on my tongue that indicated it was the same instant stuff I could buy at the grocery store for a few cents per pouch. This reassured me that the pittance I'd been charged for it was enough of a markup for this place to make some profit.

"She put her hands on mine and burned the humanity out of me, much like I burned the vampirism out of you. You don't want any more fries?"

I glanced down at the carton, took a couple more, dunked them in ketchup, and ate them, tasting their salty, greasy goodness. "So that's how someone becomes an angel?"

"When it works, yeah." He shrugged.

"What do you mean, when it works?"

"Not everyone can ascend. When one of my kind touches tainted flesh, we're risking our lives. I mean, we're only immortal in that we can live indefinitely. It doesn't mean we can't be killed. Same as a vampire." He bit deep into his burger again.

"But… you touched me," I said. "Isn't my flesh tainted worse than a regular human's?"

"Mmm-hmm," he said with his mouth full. Then he swallowed. "And it worked. Which is really interesting."

"You risked *death* to save me tonight?" Now I really was squeezing my hot chocolate and had to pry my fingers free before the cardboard cup collapsed. I placed my hands flat on the table.

21

"Why would you risk death for me?" I demanded.

"To see what would happen," Corban said before cramming the rest of the burger into his mouth. The color was returning to his cheeks, which indicated to me that he was feeding on more than just that hamburger.

"Are you insane?"

He finished chewing, drank some more soda, and sat back. "Look, once you get past a certain age, you come to terms with the fact that you'll probably die at some point, and a good death is better than a meaningless life."

"Your life isn't meaningless. You're responsible for Taos and... wherever else you..." I gestured vaguely. "You know... patrol. And if it's so hard to make more of your kind, you can't just throw your life away."

He looked right at me and, for several heartbeats, said nothing, then he leaned forward and rested his hands on the table. "So, let me explain how this works. My kind, we communicate with God the same way your kind does. We pray. We try to find signs. We follow our own hearts about what's right and what's wrong and we think every day about the big questions of good and evil."

I let that sink in. "I guess I thought you'd have a more direct line to the guy upstairs."

"You really think that you, a child of God, would be given a second-rate way to communicate with Him?"

"It… doesn't always feel like a great way to communicate," I said. "I thought there might be better. And I thought you guys were supposed to be visitors from heaven."

"I'm not that kind of angel. Members of my order are probably pretty low ranking in the grand scheme of things. Read the Bible and you'll know there are a whole lotta types of celestial beings. And no, I haven't seen any of the others. As far as a better form of communication? Maybe in the afterlife, but not here. It's a fallen world. Being just out of God's reach is kind of the whole point of this place and my role, as best as I can tell, is to be right here with you." His gaze was downright intense.

I forced myself to return it, wondering what his point was.

He leaned in closer. "Now, when I see something that I've always been told is a demon looking back at me, able to see me when no demon should, that's a sign of something. Not necessarily a good something, but when I find that supposed demon hasn't won yet, but is still locked in a war with a human soul for its body, and when that human is pure enough in heart for me to endure her touch, then that's a whole lot of signs. I can't say for sure what your purpose is in all this. I'm not even sure the rest of my kind would agree with me about helping you, but I'm the one in this position, not them. You were put in my path, not theirs. You're fighting a war no mortal has ever won, and you probably won't win it either, but if I can help you, I will. Or else I've got a long, long time to spend agonizing over what if." His blue eyes were steady and his gaze piercing.

It became more than I could endure, so I looked down, then drank some more hot chocolate. "And if I go around telling people that you can be killed with a touch?" Now the way he'd reacted when we first met, ducking away from my hands, made sense.

"Some of my kind might blame me for telling you our secret, but I'm a big believer in the power of free will. I'd blame you." He winked, like he found this funny.

I certainly did not, but I hid my confusion by drinking more hot chocolate.

"You sure you don't want any more fries?" he asked.

"I believe fries are a temptation of the devil," I said. "Worst thing I could put in my body."

He laughed. "Oh, I dunno. I take it you've never tried arsenic." But despite his amusement, he gathered up the rest of his fries and got to work eating them.

"So anyone could kill you with a touch to the skin?" I asked.

I expected him to refuse to answer, but he drank more soda and said, "It depends on where I'm touched. The thicker my skin, the less damage it does. Touch me on my shoulder or something and I have plenty of time to break your hold. Touch me where the skin is thinner…" He held up his palms. "Then I'm more vulnerable."

"Does it matter how thin my skin is where you touched me?" I asked.

He nodded. "So holding the backs of your hands like I did, way less painful than palm to palm. Unless you've got major calluses."

"Well, if you didn't want to hold hands…" I said, letting my voice trail off. That was a lame joke.

But he smiled. "Don't take it personally. It also depends on the condition of whoever's touching me. The weaker they are, the less damage they do."

"So you can hands-on heal a person who's very sick?" I asked.

"Sometimes. In special cases. Yes. And sometimes they don't survive, per se, but ascend instead."

I sat back and tried to process it all. Even in this last week, when I'd wondered every morning if death was around the corner and suspected an angel was a phone call away, I hadn't put much thought into facing the divine.

This moment was much weirder than I felt equipped to deal with. Did it show? Did he pity me? If so, he did a good job of hiding it. His demeanor indicated that he thought we were friends, even though we barely knew each other and were at literal opposite ends of the moral spectrum.

He dragged his last fry through the pool of ketchup and ate it, then wadded up all the trash left over from his meal.

I'd also expected an angel to act a little more above it all than this guy, who ate fast food and cracked snarky jokes. "How old are you?" I asked.

"I dunno. Old." He held out a hand for my cup.

I drained the last of my hot chocolate and handed it to him, careful not to touch his skin. "Where were you when you were sentenced to die? I mean, who does public sacrifices these days?"

"Does anyone? I was in north Africa." He slid out of his seat to throw away the trash and I slid out of mine as well, to follow him. Apparently he was all done with his feeding.

"So you got sentenced by who? ISIS?" I asked.

He laughed. "No."

"Then who?"

"The Romans." He dumped our trash and headed towards the door.

I stayed right on his heels, and we pushed our way out into the chill night air.

"The Romans?" I asked.

He paused to look around, then turned to me. "I was converted to Christianity by Paul."

Paul? That name plus the reference to Romans took a moment for me to piece together. "The Apostle Paul?" I asked. "The guy who started out as Saul on the road to Damascus?"

"That's the guy. He converted a lot of people." He shrugged again, casually, but the illusion I had of him had shattered. He'd gone from being a teenager with supernatural issues like me to something completely alien.

"You're two thousand years old?"

"Something like that. And before you ask, no, I don't think I ever met anyone else who got written up in the Bible." Again with the shrug as he pulled his gloves back on.

My head was spinning. "So who's your superior? I mean… are there many angels older than Christianity?"

"Christianity didn't invent us," he said. "Not even Christians think that. But look, I'm not gonna answer questions that delve into that kind of thing. My kind doesn't call balls and strikes on the religions people practice or what they believe about religious history. That's a minefield. And I'm not gonna tell you what makes one of my kind stronger than another or have more authority. That's all a trade secret."

"Are some of your kind not Christians?" I asked.

He only smiled in reply. It was clear he'd stick to his guns on this point.

I heaved a sigh, my breath steaming in the air. "Well, you look good for your age," I quipped.

That earned me a laugh. "Thanks. The thing is, I may have been alive all this time, but I haven't really lived all of it, if you know what I mean."

"No," I said. "I have no idea what you mean."

He chuckled again. "You ever zone out during a boring lecture?"

"Well… maybe…" I had both a reputation for honesty and a reputation as a nerd to protect here, so it was hard to craft a good answer.

"If you live long enough, life becomes like a boring lecture. As much as you try to stay involved and to care, it becomes a blur. I do care about people, but I know better than to get too invested in them. Some succeed, some fail, and they all die. The same is true with civilizations, technology... In an absolute sense, there's very little that is ever new in this world." He looked down at me, once again giving me the sense that we were friends. That he was comfortable having me know who and what he was.

I looked down at my boots. "I'm guessing high school for the five-hundredth time doesn't hold your interest."

"No, it does not. And I was never a scholar anyway. The thing is, by the time I met you, I'd been on autopilot so long that I forgot what living felt like. You kind of knocked me out of my groove there, which is a good thing. I'm grateful. Can I drive you home and can we talk about Evan, now?"

I did want to go home, and I definitely wanted to talk about Evan, so I nodded.

He unlocked his car with his key fob. At least I didn't have to drive this time.

"How long until Evan and his sire get to town?" I asked.

"I'm guessing they're already here. That's why I need to talk to you now."

22

"Sooo," said Corban, as he turned the car onto the main road, "here's the thing about vampires. There are never very many of them at any one time. Unless there's a major outbreak, I see one pop up maybe once a decade or so."

"But you said there are more of them since people started thinking of them as sexy," I said. The night had that velvety quality to the darkness, broken only by the occasional street light.

"Yeah, but by that I mean I've seen thirty in the last twenty years. Most of the ones I see are babies. Turned within the last few months, like Evan."

"But you only cover the Taos region," I said. "Thirty here sounds like a lot."

He shook his head. "When it comes to vampires, other members of my order call on me to go help out. Because of my age, and because vamps are so deadly and dangerous. I've killed a few hundred so that kind of makes me an expert."

I stared at him. "I thought you were a vampire hunter."

"I am."

"As, like, your main job."

He shook his head. "No, it was just my main reason for dealing with you the way I did. I didn't think my work with humans pertained."

"And so being a good vampire hunter doesn't make you all that high ranking in your organization?"

"I'm not answering that, all right? You already know more than any vampire's ever been told by one of my kind."

That was fair. "Okay," I said. "So how do you kill vampires?"

"I'm not going to tell you all the ways in case you turn. I need some element of surprise."

I nodded. Because calmly accepting a guy telling me he needed to be able to kill me whenever he wanted was now my normal.

"Sunlight works," he said. "Decapitation works. Stabbing the heart can theoretically work too, but it's really hard to do. You ever tried to punch through a human sternum?"

I stared at him. Silence descended, but for the sound of the car engine and the tires rolling on asphalt.

He glanced back at me. "What?"

"What do *you* think?"

"Well, in biology class or–"

"We don't dissect people in biology."

"All right, all right–"

"And I don't know what kind of dissection you've been doing, but punching through–"

"All *right*," he cut me off, eyes twinkling. "Fine. Suffice it to say, it's hard to do. Back in the olden days people would chain the vamp down and drive the stake with a sledgehammer. It's not my go-to method. Anyway, this isn't specifically what I wanted to talk to you about." He looked over at me, as if to check that I was listening.

Was this the kind of conversation anyone zoned out from? I met his gaze and he looked at the road again.

"There are a few nests of old vampires," he said. "Actually, these days there's just one."

"Is it in Romania?" I joked.

"No, we cleaned that one out about a century ago. It's the one in New England. There are three old, old vampires that go off-grid for centuries at a time. Really hard to kill because they've learned quite a few tricks in their lifetimes."

"And Darissa is one of them?"

"Bingo."

I stared out at the road slipping past under the beams of the headlights. We'd reached the end of town and were headed out towards the gorge. "There are three?" I asked. "I thought they tended to go in pairs."

He nodded. "Pretty much all new vamps are turned by a lover, and if that lover has a living sire there's a fight to the death and all that. Nests usually crop up when there's a different circumstance. Like in Romania it was a count and his court. They all took lovers, but the core group weren't love rivals. In New England it's three sisters, all turned by their mother before she got killed by a love rival. Darissa's the youngest one."

I pressed my fingertips to the cold glass of the window. "So you've almost eradicated vampires."

"Yes… we've been here before, though. The thing is, when they want to expand their numbers, they can do it fast."

"Oh."

"And Darissa especially gets very, very aggressive when she's angry."

"Lucky me," I said.

"Right? She's reckless and impetuous, but she's smart, too. I've hunted her two separate times and she always gives me the slip. Usually getting rid of the lovers she and her siblings turn is the best we can do."

"How old is she?" I asked.

"Mmmm… we're not sure if she was turned in New England or North America for that matter. If she was, then she'd obviously be four hundred some odd years old, but I'd guess she's older. She and her siblings look like they're from southern Europe. Definitely not Native American. If they were turned in Europe and came over, then there's not really any way to know. Like I said, they go off the grid for long periods of time, and who knows how many times they've changed their names and identities. We call her Darissa because it's the name she had when she first came on our radar a few centuries ago."

I watched his profile as he spoke. He shot me the occasional sidelong look.

"How do they stay off-grid if they have to feed?" I asked. When I'd been Evan's food source, the marks on my neck were pretty distinctive looking. Human bites, even when the humans had long canines, weren't going to be mistaken for any other kind of animal bite. They were an odd crescent shape.

"Probably they take some people hostage and farm them," said Corban. "Until they get bored or their supply of humans runs out or gets too inbred."

That thought made my skin crawl. Life was hard enough while I was enslaved to vampirism. I didn't want to imagine life enslaved to actual vampires, kept for nothing more than food, unable to see the outside world. A chill went down my spine and I pulled my jacket still tighter around myself. "Has Darissa killed any of your kind?" I asked.

"Yep."

"How many?"

He paused, took a deep breath, then said, "About a dozen. She's a mean one. But here's the thing, when she's out in the world, she's vulnerable. Just setting traps for her and such doesn't work if we've got nothing she wants. If she's risking exposure, she wants something."

"She wants Evan, apparently."

Corban shook his head. "She wants you. She'd ditch Evan in a heartbeat. Lovers aren't great bait with her. Even love rivals usually aren't, but apparently you matter enough to draw her all the way out here."

We'd been driving long enough that I wondered if we'd already crossed the bridge. In the darkness, it wasn't possible to see the gorge, and I hadn't paid close enough attention to note whether we'd passed the section of road with guardrails. The supernatural horrors we discussed were distracting me from natural ones.

"So I'm the bait?" I asked.

Corban didn't answer immediately. He took a few breaths, then said, "I was trying to take them on by myself, but when you called, I knew I had to come back."

"For the sake of Taos."

He lifted one shoulder at that. "Sure, okay, but this place doesn't self-destruct without me. It just gets more chaotic. I came back for you, to see if I could help you stay human. Once I broke off the chase, Evan and Darissa will have come straight here."

"Oh."

He looked over at me. "Listen. You and I are going to work together and we'll either eliminate Darissa or drive her back into hiding. I'm not going to use you as bait, all right? We'll just work with the knowledge that you're what she wants."

"Do your kind usually work in teams on a project like this?"

"Sometimes." He inclined his head as if this were a minor detail.

"And are you able to call in more of your kind, or is that not possible because they might want to kill me, or use me as bait, then kill me?"

This time he took his eyes off the road for a full second to look at me.

I chewed my lip and stared at the darkness outside my window.

"I've hunted her with teams of my kind before," Corban said, finally looking back at the road. "It's never worked, so changing it up isn't the worst idea."

Changing it up so that he was working with a weaker, lesser being didn't seem like brilliant planning to me.

He kept talking, though, "Darissa's well out of her element here. I've never known her to range this far from her nest."

"She must really hate me, then."

"I guess. So... can you tell me about Evan?"

"Hot, popular guy," I said. "Kind of a player. Didn't ever do commitment."

"I'm more interested in why he turned you. I know you may still not be comfortable talking about it, but I need to know what the deal is. Anything you can tell me."

I leaned against the door and for a moment reflected on how only a few sheets of metal and door-handle mechanics stood between me and the certain death by falling onto the asphalt at high speed. Or maybe I'd turn at the last second.

What Corban asked was fair. I shut my eyes and sent my memory back.

23

Evan had been extra jumpy that last night when he'd fed on me. He'd woken me up from a deep sleep, his ice-cold hands on the bare skin of my arms. I had wondered how he'd gotten into my room; now I knew he'd likely used his mist form.

"Lia," he whispered. "Lia, wake up."

I'd dragged myself from the depths of unconsciousness and lay blinking up at the ceiling for a long moment while reality coalesced around me. Evan was seated on the edge of my bed, looking down at me.

"Hey," I said, sleepily.

"I need you to promise me something." His gray eyes looked ghostly in the darkness.

"Mmmm?"

"Don't invite anyone new into your room, okay?"

I stretched and sat up. "Okay."

"The girl who turned me, she's back. She found me, and she says I belong with her."

I nodded. Then it began to sink in that she was a vampire, and I realized I wasn't equipped to deal with her if she came after me.

"Lia, I don't want to be with her. I want to be with you."

On one level, my heart soared, but on another, reality intruded. Of course he preferred me. I was easier to manipulate, more malleable. This wasn't love. It was convenience.

"Do you want to be with me?" he asked. He'd kept his hands on my arms this whole time, his skin warming from the contact with mine.

It wasn't as if I could say no. Despite my resentment at all the compromises I'd made for him, I was hooked. Intellectually I knew our relationship wasn't healthy, but emotionally I was all in.

"Do you?" he pressed. His pupils were dilating. His methods for keeping me in his thrall might have been wrong, but the desire he felt for me looked real, and I couldn't see past that.

"Yeah," I whispered.

"Then let me turn you. You're smart, Lia. If you were also a vampire, you could figure out how to get away from this girl. Can I turn you?"

I rubbed my eyes, unable to fully wrap my head around what he was asking me. Vampirism didn't fit in with my plans to go to Princeton and eventually become an investment banker. Then again, neither did spending my last semester of high school so drained of energy that it was all I could do to maintain my GPA.

So it was a purely emotional decision when I nodded. I didn't think it through, and I didn't have time to reconsider before Evan slashed his own palm and pressed the cut to my lips.

Drinking blood is gross. Even the memory of it made me want to gag, but I managed to swallow a few drops, and then Evan fed on me, wrapping his arms around me. I lay back in bed, and had let him drain me until I lost consciousness.

BY NOW WE'D reached Aunt Cassie's driveway. Corban pulled in, parked, and turned his full attention to me. "Then what happened?" he asked.

"Nothing." I said. "I woke up in the morning, feeling like my skin was on fire and that made me realize I'd done something incredibly stupid. I didn't get out of the sunlight because I figured I'd rather die than be a vampire. When the burning stopped I looked at myself in the mirror and I was all… different. Prettier."

He nodded.

But I couldn't look at him. "You say I'm strong," I said. "I'm not. I was weak, and I ended up half-turned like this because I was so weak that I couldn't face what I'd done to myself."

For several heartbeats, Corban didn't reply. My own breaths and the almost silent thrum of the engine were the only sounds to fill that infinite silence.

Finally, he said, "You can have moments of weakness and still be strong, you know that?"

"In theory," I replied. "But that's not me."

"Well… I hear what you're saying about feeling ashamed of letting Evan manipulate you, but it takes strength to face down a decision like you did that morning. Most people would have given in to the pain, hidden from the sun and let the vampirism control the rest of their existence. Most people wouldn't have decided that death was better than a life enslaved."

I had not felt any of those noble feelings when I'd let the sun burn me. This was the second time in the last couple of months that I had a guy telling me how I really was. Evan had espoused the view that I was meant for him and that I wasn't the strong, independent woman I'd always believed I was.

Corban thought the opposite. The problem was, even if Corban believed I was the person I wished I was, I couldn't let his opinion matter too much.

I turned to him. "Thanks," I said, "but it's not for you to say how I really am."

His smile was knowing. "Exactly right. Just, for what it's worth? There's a reason why a lot of principled people have strict rules to keep themselves from temptation. It's not weak to know your weaknesses. That's strength."

I wondered if he was digging at me for refusing to be alone in my room with him.

But he changed the subject back to what mattered now. "What happened after the sun burned you that first morning?"

"I got up and got on with my day. I never saw Evan again. Typical situation of a guy bailing once he got what he wanted."

"Except he didn't. He lost you as a food source and never got your help. I'm guessing his sire got to him before he could find you again."

Perhaps, but I didn't care what Evan's reasons were for bailing on me. "What's your plan to deal with him and Darissa?"

"Well…" he said, "Evan's waiting by your window. First step is for you to talk to him and gather information. See if anything's changed about what he wants."

"He's outside my window?" I felt a jolt of panic.

Corban nodded. "They move fast in the dark, vampires. They kind of don't care about speed limits. Darissa dumped him off here and took the car."

"But… he's… is Cassie okay?"

"Yeah, the spell on the house is holding fine. I need you to go to talk to Evan."

I bit my lip. "Can you come in with me and just stay out of sight while I talk to him?"

Corban looked away. "I'd rather not."

"Why not?" I said. "You want me to face down a vampire on my own?"

"No, I'd rather you didn't talk to him at all, but this moment isn't about me and what I want."

"Excuse me?" I said. I did not get what his issue was. This guy was supposed to be a superior being, and I got the impression right now that he was being petty.

He looked sidelong at me. "First of all, I don't want to risk being seen by Evan. I mean, I don't think he'd be able to see me because I've seen no evidence of that, but since he's your sire and you can see me, it's theoretically possible. It wouldn't be the first time Darissa faked not having an advantage. Besides, when I think of what that guy did to you, I want to kill him. Just end his existence as fast as possible, but he's a key to Darissa and Darissa is dangerous. Do me a favor and don't make me endure watching him manipulate you."

"You want me to pray to your boss about this and just muddle through?"

"I'll be here, okay? I've got ways of watching over the situation as it unfolds."

I wanted to press the point, but I reminded myself that I'd gotten myself into this situation and Corban had already risked his life once tonight for me. His refusal to back me up confused me, but a lot of things about him confused me. Given he was two thousand years old, that shouldn't have been surprising.

I also knew deep down that I'd argued because I didn't want to face Evan and my terrible choices with him again. I opened my door and got out.

24

Aunt Cassie was sitting in the kitchen, in the dark, fidgeting.

Great. I was dealing with a stonewalling angel in the driveway, a needy vampire outside my window, and now a guardian who wasn't doing the necessary adulting to be a guardian.

I switched on the light. "Hi," I said to my aunt.

At least she was dressed and not in that bathrobe. She wore a tie-dyed shirt and tie-dyed leggings that didn't go together, and had her hair up in a messy bun. When the light came on, she startled and blinked at me. After her eyes adjusted, she held up what looked like part of a scarf that she was crocheting. "Can you turn the lights out?" she asked.

"You're learning to crochet in the dark?" I asked.

"I already know how to crochet. The dark makes it more interesting."

"So, in case you go blind, you can still make scarves?"

"Sure. I suppose that's one application. You're in a mood tonight."

"I left my extra tamales in Gina's car."

"And Corban drove you home."

So she wasn't completely out of it. Corban's car was easy to see out the window, though I didn't look at it for any longer than necessary. Cassie, as if sensing my turmoil, pulled the blinds shut.

"Don't invite anyone into the house tonight," I said over my shoulder as I headed into my room.

"Is something wrong? Did Corban hurt you?"

I paused in my doorway and looked back at her, feeling instantly guilty for my cavalier attitude. Yes, she was a kook, but she still cared about me, and she kept her own life together well enough. In this moment, she sat wearing the clothes she wanted in the bizarro kitchen of the house she wanted. I'd be lucky to accomplish that much in what was left of my life.

And there was a very dangerous bloodsucking demon lurking nearby who would kill her if given the chance. I wasn't sure how I knew Evan had abandoned all human ethics, even the dictate not to kill people, but I knew.

"No," I said. "Corban's fine."

"All right. And why shouldn't I invite anyone in?"

I weighed possible answers for a moment, then settled on: "My ex-boyfriend may have come to town to find me."

"Are you serious?"

"Yeah… I mean, I haven't seen him. I've just heard he might be here." I hoped against hope that she wouldn't press me on where I'd heard this.

"Well," said Cassie, "let me know what you need." She meant it too, even if she couldn't promise to provide for said needs.

"Thanks," I said. I went the rest of the way into my room, shut the door, and took a good look around. Had I really gawked at Amy's bedroom earlier that day? At least hers had square walls and a place to hang clothing. Mine looked like the inside of an alien seed pod and the only clothing storage was in a low cabinet made of knotty wood that didn't really fit together. I pulled open one of the doors, got down on my knees, and dug around until I found my manicure kit.

Then I turned off the main light, turned on my little bedside light, pulled my chair over to the window, grabbed the garbage can, and got to work cutting my toenails, with the window opened just a crack, letting frigid air stream in.

Here went nothing. In the void where my guilt about Dad's death should have been had poured a firm batch of resolve. I was ready to take revenge in any way possible. I looked inward at the razor blade of grief lodged by my heart and let the pain flow, except rather than get sad, I got angry. The person responsible for killing my father and ruining my life was nearby, and I was about to face him. None of this would have happened if not for Evan.

Sure enough, a form coalesced outside, and despite everything that had already happened this evening, my heart pounded like it wanted to bust out of my chest. I doubted I'd ever get used to seeing supernatural stuff, and I fantasized about one day having a life when I didn't have to.

"Lia?" Evan said. He stood, looking a far cry from the thin, gaunt, and pale creature he'd been the first time he ever fed on me. Instead he looked how he had before he'd turned, though maybe paler. He wore a plain, dark-colored t-shirt that made no sense given the chill temperatures. Apparently vampires didn't have to keep warm, though I wondered if the low temperatures slowed them down at all.

As angry as I was with him and as bad as I knew he was for me, my heart still lurched at the sight of him. My weak, traitorous heart remembered what it was like to kiss him, to lie with our bodies intertwined, to have him tell me that he cared about me. Loved me. He clearly didn't need me to feed on anymore, and yet he was still here. He'd come a long way to find me.

And probably kill me, I reminded myself.

I was halfway through trimming my big toenail, though, so I took my time to finish, collecting my thoughts as I did. "Liana," I said, keeping my voice even. "My name's Liana."

"Right, Liana then." His tone was hesitant. "How are you?"

"Not happy that you followed me." It was easier not to look at him, so I didn't.

"I had to find you. You may think I abandoned you the night after you turned, but I didn't, okay? I was captured. I fought as hard as I could to get away and come to you but..."

I paused in my clipping and looked at him. He was here because Darissa forced him to be and he just wanted to save himself. This had always been about him saving himself.

Corban was the antithesis. While this boy had used me to feed, Corban had risked himself to save me. But I shouldn't compare them, because it wasn't like I could date Corban.

I resumed clipping my toenails, refusing to let the feeling that I was being ridiculous dominate. Evan waited outside until I got tired of hearing silence punctuated by snips.

"I'm not inviting you in," I said.

"How are you not a vampire? I mean… when I left you, I thought you were dead. No pulse, stone-cold skin. I thought I'd killed you until Darissa told me different." There was real anguish in his voice.

Most people, I reminded myself, *would be anguished at the thought of killing anyone.* This wasn't evidence of him truly caring about me. I made myself shrug the way Corban did when brushing off matters of life and death. There was no need to get into details about being half turned. The less information he had about me, the better. "What do you want?"

"To get away from Darissa."

I didn't want to let on that I knew about his sire. "And who's Darissa?" I finished clipping the last toenail and set my clippers aside.

"That girl. The vampire. The one who turned me."

"In other words," I said, "your problem, not mine."

"No, she wants me to capture you so that she can torture and kill you in front of me."

I got to my feet and looked him in the eye. It wasn't something I would have dared to do before he turned, or even while he fed on me, and even now it wasn't easy. In my mind's eye, I tried to picture myself standing tall and defiant. In reality, I just stood. That was challenging enough. Evan was the kind of guy who could make me feel two inches tall with a sneer. I'd just never known that before he started looking at me.

"You going to do that?" I asked. "You going to capture me and take me to her."

"No. I wouldn't have told you if I was going to do that, would I?"

"Wow... that's really big of you."

"Liana, I'm sorry okay? Truly."

"Who've you been feeding on?"

He shrugged. "No one person. Nobody who mattered."

"Just whoever was convenient?"

He rolled his eyes like I was being irrational. "Nobody I formed a relationship with, okay? Listen, let me turn you for reals this time and then let's take down Darissa. We can be together forever, then. Or not. Whatever you want."

Even while dazzled by his good looks and attention, I could tell that he wouldn't do "whatever" I wanted. Any girl who tried to sign up for forever with him would end up doing whatever *he* wanted. He was here at my window because of what he wanted.

He looked me in the eye and his shoulders bowed slightly. "Please," he said. "She's... you have no idea how she is."

25

Seeing Evan hurt always made me want to hold him. Well, ever since our relationship, if what we had merited that term, at least. I made myself remember all the times he'd forced things against my will. He did not deserve my pity. I wasn't inviting him into my room for good reason. He belonged out in the cold.

"Well," I said, "if Darissa's hurt you, then I really am sorry to hear that."

"Yeah…" He folded his arms over his chest and kept his head bowed as he looked at me. He could read all the things I wasn't saying from the few things that I was.

I was actually getting to him. It felt like I was a superwoman.

"Where is Darissa right now?" I asked.

"Back at the hotel. I mean, if we work together tonight, we've got time to come up with a plan to defeat her."

"How do you figure?" I folded my arms.

"I don't know exactly what to do, but you're smart. I figured you'd have ideas."

I rolled my eyes. "You went to the same fancy prep school that I did. Weren't you planning to go to Stanford?"

"You were the top student at the school."

"Was," I said. "Until you started sucking the life out of me, got my father killed, and sent me off into hiding."

He looked down. "Yeah, I'm sorry about that."

"Are you? Or are you just sorry that I'm not going to help you out again?"

He kept his gaze fixed on his feet. "No, I really am sorry. Everything that's happened since that party... it's so messed up. I didn't mean to pull you down with me. But this can totally work to our advantage. We're immortal. Who cares about college when you have eternity, right?"

I took a moment to look him over once again, mainly because I was amazed at how it made him squirm. "I have no interest in spending eternity with you." That wasn't entirely true. I had some interest, but I was adopting the fake-it-until-you-make-it approach this time around. Rather than think about what I wanted right now, I thought about the regret I'd felt all those mornings after.

Evan shut his eyes and leaned against the window frame, looking the very picture of desperate. "Lia..."

"Liana."

"She'll kill you. Unless you find a way to kill her. And I'll help you kill her, okay? Even if we go our separate ways after."

"Who did you feed on? I'm not asking because I'm jealous. I'm asking because I'd like to know exactly what price you and your kind pay for eternity."

He looked past me. "Nobody… nobody who mattered."

"How many of those nobodies have you killed?"

"Liana, the world isn't always sunshine and rainbows and unicorns."

"Because those are totally the two options," I said. "Sunshine, rainbows, and unicorns or sucking the life out of the one person who tried to help you when you were starving and then killing others for food. For your information, I don't even like unicorns." What I didn't have in courage, I made up for by being pedantic. It was a matter of playing to my strengths.

"Okay," he relented, "so what are you going to do when Darissa comes after you?"

"Whatever amazing plan you thought I'd come up with tonight," I said, shutting the window and drawing the curtain. I needed to shut him out before the conversation went on much longer. I felt like I was on a winning streak–or at least a not-being-steamrollered-by-the-hot-guy streak. I needed to quit while I was ahead.

"Liana, she really will kill you. I can help you. I know all about her."

He thought I was going this alone, and that was good. He hadn't seen Corban. I turned away from the window. While I still didn't know Corban that well, I did know that I couldn't try to form an alliance with Evan. I really was a rules girl.

I kept the little interior light on so that I wouldn't be able to see Evan's silhouette against the curtains, and I hoped against hope that the protection spell on my room really was active.

With a shove, I put my garbage can back by the bed and quickly changed into my pajamas.

Then I realized that for the first time in a week, I was exhausted. Tomorrow was a school day and I needed sleep. I turned out the lights, took a deep breath, opened the curtains again, and found Evan gone. Not that it mattered, I decided. He could look in if he wanted to. I had a date with sunrise, and despite the prospect of a demon lurking around my house, I actually managed to fall asleep pretty fast.

I AWOKE TO the usual morning burn, but it was back to the level it had been before Corban left. I still felt like molten metal was pouring over my body, but not that I was about to rupture and die.

Once it passed, I heard the sound of someone tapping at my window. Corban leaned against the outside of the house, shielding his eyes so that he could peer in.

"Hey," I said as I pushed the window open, hard enough to knock him back half a step. "Don't come looking in my window." Cold air rushed in so I quickly hauled him in with a grip on the front of his jacket and closed the window behind him.

"You didn't close the curtains," he said.

"I had to let the sunshine in, and..." I gestured past him at the great expanse of Taos Valley. There were a couple of Earthships in the distance, but they weren't close enough for people to see in my window. "For all you know, I coulda been sleeping in the nude, and what would that have done to your divine reputation?" I wasn't in the nude, of course. I was in a nightshirt and leggings that, now that I looked down at them, reminded me of the kind of clothing Cassie had been wearing last night, minus the tie-dye.

"If I'd seen you in the nude," said Corban. "I think you'd be more embarrassed than me. You've studied ancient Greece, haven't you?"

I stalked over to my bathrobe and wrapped it around myself. At least it wasn't bleach-stained, stiff terry cloth. It was pink silk with cherry blossoms. "Were you out there all night?"

"I followed Evan after he left. He didn't dare go back to Darissa. He hid in a little cave."

"A cave?"

"A tiny hollow under a rock so there's no easy way to collapse it and expose him to the sun. He got a lot of practice at finding hiding places in the desert this week, but things are different this close to a town. I can get a little mini backhoe–"

"You can?" I looked over at him.

"Yeah, you can rent them from the hardware store. I'll go get a mini backhoe and go dig him out this morning. You want to join me?"

"Um..."

"I'd rather have you with me while Darissa's around. Just in case she makes a move. I couldn't figure out where she's gone at the moment, so you're in danger anywhere indoors, without sunlight."

I did not want to face her alone, and I still felt somewhat responsible for Evan, so it didn't seem right to make Corban go deal with him on his own. "Okay. So what I learned from Evan last night was–"

"Darissa wants to capture you alive," said Corban. "Yeah, I heard. That's interesting."

"Do you know why she'd want to capture me?"

A crash in the kitchen interrupted us. "Cassie's not in a great mood," he said. "And before you ask, no, I'm not feeding on her."

Her mood was clear from the noise she was making.

I pushed Corban toward the window. "Go around to the door," I said. Cassie said she didn't care, but I was not brave enough to stride out of my bedroom with a guy on my heels first thing in the morning. Belatedly, I remembered he could do his invisibility thing.

But he was already halfway out the window.

This made for a long pause in the conversation while I cranked the window shut and then went to open the back door, while Cassie fussed with the coffeemaker. Corban ducked in along with another blast of cold air.

Cassie turned, looked at him, looked at me, and headed downstairs.

"Um–" I began.

"Don't ask me for permission. Do what you want," she said.

Corban shrugged.

"Do you want food?" I asked her.

"No."

I looked at Corban.

"I'm good," he said.

"We have Pop Tarts."

He lowered his voice. "Those aren't food. Seriously, I eat maybe once every five years and I can tell you that." He sat down at the table, where Cassie had been sitting last night, and leaned back.

"If you kept Pop Tarts around you wouldn't have to restock every five years," I pointed out. "One box can last you fifteen or twenty years, easily."

"Gross."

I put some bread in the toaster and finished getting the coffeepot going.

"Aunt Cassie?" I called out. "Can you excuse me from school this morning?"

"You're eighteen," she shouted back. "Excuse yourself!"

I looked at Corban. "Can I do that?"

"Why wouldn't you be able to?" he asked. "You're a legal adult."

"But that's… weird."

He shrugged.

I called the office, though, and said that I had some business with my dad's death to deal with, which was technically true. The secretary noted down my excuse and that was that. I couldn't help but stare at my phone after we'd hung up. This was another result, I suspected, of not celebrating my birthday. Not marking the milestone meant getting surprised with stuff like this.

Corban was tapping away on his phone, totally missing this mind-blowing moment.

"I need to make another pot of coffee," I said, "and then we can go."

Go try to kill my ex-boyfriend, I thought, *because that's my life now.*

26

I wasn't sure which was more disturbing, being able to get myself out of school or being able to rent a mini backhoe. A person could do a lot of damage with a backhoe.

Focusing on this list of choices allowed me not to think about the truly disturbing part of this morning, attempting to kill Evan. Yes, he'd admitted last night that he'd killed people, and yes, I knew he'd keep doing it. That didn't make this easy. So I focused on how disturbing it was that I could rent a backhoe, that could be used to kill all kinds of things if one were unscrupulous.

That said, I wasn't sure I was old enough to rent it myself. Corban handled that and I had no idea what age was printed on his driver's license.

All I knew was that half an hour later we were towing a mini backhoe on a trailer behind his RAV4. "This," he said, "is why I got one with a V6 engine."

"Yeah," I said. "I'll pretend to know what you're talking about."

As usual, he laughed like I'd made some witty joke. The trailer bounced over the rough road as we hauled it out of town, across the gorge, and back into my aunt's subdivision.

"Wait," I said. "Are we going to have to rip up someone else's property to do this?" This too was diversion. Caring about the damage my ex's death might cause to landscaping.

"Mmm-hmm," he said. "But the property owner is out of town."

"How does that make it okay?"

"It means we can put off making up an excuse until after, once we see how much damage we do."

"Right…" I said.

I felt useless as we pulled over at one of the countless big lots in the subdivision and Corban unloaded the backhoe from the trailer. He drove it over to a flat boulder that I would never have realized had a hollow under it big enough for a person to hide in.

While Corban braced the backhoe and began to dig out the boulder, I tried not to be an utter basket case. I was literally watching a murder in progress. Evan was dead, I reminded myself, but the version of him I'd been involved with wasn't. Evan was a killer. The fact that he hadn't killed me didn't exonerate him.

With a metallic screech, Corban got the boulder levered up and pushed to the side, leaving an open hole underneath. There was no sign of Evan other than some shoe prints.

Corban jumped down from the backhoe and went to look, though I noticed he kept his distance. "Yeah," he said, "I thought that might be the case. He's too smart to stay where he could be trapped like that. There's a prairie dog town here."

I stared at him. "What?"

"You know what prairie dogs are?"

"Those little rodent things?" I hazarded. "Look like brown squirrels with no tails?" I'd seen them at the zoo before. "They live in towns?"

"Yeah, the big old maze of tunnels they make is called a town, so I'm guessing he popped into mist form and went into those tunnels." He pointed to a small hole at the back of the hollow under the boulder.

"Soooo… do you keep digging?"

He shook his head. "Mist form takes energy. He already spent a lot being in mist form by your window and hasn't eaten since then, so he won't be able to hold it for long now. It's only a matter of time before he pops back into his regular body."

"And then what?" I asked.

"Boom, probably. I'm not sure."

"Boom?"

Right then, the entire ground in front of us erupted. One moment I was standing on firm footing, and the next I was being hauled back by Corban, his hands gripping me under my arms. The air filled with dust, making my eyes and throat itch so bad that I couldn't stop coughing.

I screwed my eyes shut and let Corban guide me back towards the car.

My ribs began to ache as the coughing fit went on and on until finally I took a deep breath of clean air. My palms were spread flat against the hood of Corban's car, and even that was covered with a good layer of dust.

"Yeah," said Corban. "Boom. Dirt and prairie dogs everywhere."

"What? Prairie dogs?" I pivoted and could only make out the still-expanding cloud of dust.

Corban wrapped an arm around my shoulders and pointed so that I could sight down his arm to a little brown rodent lying asleep on the ground. "They were hibernating," he said.

I hid my eyes. "Are there babies?"

"What?"

"Are their babies born over the winter, during hibernation? Like bears?"

"Um… I don't see any babies. Here…" He let me go and got out his phone. "No. They give birth in the spring, not while hibernating."

I exhaled. "Okay. Did we kill any?"

"I dunno. They all look asleep. Well, that one's moving. They're groggy, that's for sure."

I hazarded another look and saw that a giant crater had opened up. Even the ground under the boulder had collapsed so that it had rolled down to the bottom. The mini backhoe had been thrown and lay on its side several yards away. Thank goodness Corban had been able to haul me out of the way of all that.

The scene was surreal, like a mini asteroid hit. Dirt was still caving in at the edges of the crater and there really were groggy prairie dogs everywhere, little brown rodents, hard to spot unless one knew what to look for, some of them scrabbling weakly. I wondered how many had been crushed under the collapsing dirt or that boulder.

I tried to think of something else. "Popping out of mist form packs a punch," I said. "How many tons of dirt do you think that is?"

"Nerd girl, why do you keep asking me stuff as if I would know? Being old isn't the same as being wise."

"Well," I retorted, "what do you think when you see something like this?"

"I think, 'Wow. I need to figure out how to explain this to the landowner.'"

There was that. "I already had that thought, though," I pointed out. "Before this."

Corban smirked at me.

Right then, Aunt Cassie came driving past. I'd been so distracted that I hadn't seen her car approaching on the flat road. Now, though, she was close enough to stop and roll down her window.

For a moment she just stared at the scene of destruction. Then she looked at me, then at Corban, then began to roll up her window.

"Hey!" I called out before she got it all the way closed.

She hesitated, then rolled it down.

"Can you call animal control or… whoever? Department of Wildlife?"

Next she'd ask what she was supposed to tell them, and I had no idea.

But that wasn't what she said. "Fine," was her reply. "I suggest you get gone in the next ten minutes."

I decided not to query why she had a specific time frame. For all I knew, she'd done weird stuff that she'd had to report to the same agency, and right then, her rule about not sharing more of our issues than strictly necessary seemed like a good one.

"Okay!" I called back.

She rolled up her window and drove off toward the main road.

I turned to ask Corban what we were going to do with the mini backhoe and found him deadlifting it back onto its treads.

Apparently angels had super strength too. I wondered if he could have hefted the boulder with his bare hands, though I realized that would have risked Evan grabbing him. Corban brushed off his hands, looked the vehicle over, then climbed into its driver's seat and started it up.

I stood by, feeling useless again as he loaded it back up on the trailer. At least I could help secure it. Then we both had to shake the dust out of our hair and clothes before getting into his car.

27

"This is gonna look really suspicious if we return the backhoe all covered with dust like this," I said.

"Is it?" asked Corban. "I don't think the damage here looks backhoe related. And I seriously doubt the police are gonna investigate this as a crime." He gestured at the crater and the dust still hanging in the air. "They'll probably be trying to classify it as some freakish natural phenomenon."

"Valid points," I agreed, though it was odd to think about ways the police would be misled. That went against my rule-bound nature.

Corban started his car, and drove over the uneven ground, toward the road.

That's when it fully hit me that we'd just killed Evan. I hadn't seen his body, but that massive explosion had been him being unable to sustain mist form. I wondered if he died without resuming his corporeal form, or if he snapped back to his corporeal form and died in the sunlight and crumbled to dust. Neither sounded like a great way to go.

Corban reached the paved road, carefully guided the car and trailer up onto it, and then sped up towards town.

I shut my eyes, a wave of nausea washing over me.

"You okay?" Corban asked.

I shook my head. "No."

He pulled over off the road and I peered through one eye and saw that we were in the parking area by the gorge, its great chasm open before us.

"What's wrong?" he asked.

"We just killed someone," I said. "I mean… I know you say he was already dead, but…"

"But you're not making an easy transition into being a cold-blooded killer? That's fair." He turned up the heat and angled the vents in my direction. Warm, vanilla-scented air streamed over my skin and lifted a few strands of hair off my face.

"For what it's worth," he said, "I don't like it either. No matter how often I've had to do it, I hate it. And also, for what it's worth, Evan's killed five people that I know of. He figured out that killing homeless and transients attracted less attention. Doesn't make it easy to off him, though."

"You're also not a cold-blooded killer?" I tried to keep my tone light.

"I dunno. I was a soldier when I was alive." He stared off at the gorge.

"You were?"

He nodded. "That's how I got in trouble. Roman soldiers had to contribute to religious sacrifices, and I refused."

"So did you ever fight in battles?"

He shut his eyes. "Don't laugh at me, but I don't remember. I mean, yes, I've fought in battles, but before I ascended? I don't know. It was a really long time ago and you've gotta understand, there wasn't just one Dark Age between then and now. I went through several. I've seen a lot of innocent people die, and most of them because they were on the wrong side of a border, were the wrong color, prayed to the wrong deities, or just plain had stuff their neighbors wanted. Stupid technicalities that cost them their freedom and their lives."

I let that sink in. "So… do you protect non-Christians?" Silently I prayed for an answer I could live with.

"Of course I do," he said.

Good, I thought.

"I protect good people, and Christians… I mean, nobody's perfect, but you know as well as I do that not everyone who wears the label believes Christ's teachings. Some of the nastiest wars I ever saw were done in God's name." He rubbed his face with his hands. "I don't protect you because you wear a cross, Liana. I protect you because you want what anyone would want. A normal life. Free of having to cause pain to others."

He made it sound so simple.

I felt his gaze on me. "You still have feelings for the guy?"

"Feelings, yes. What kind of feelings? I don't know. I mean, I hate what he did to me and I can't forgive him for getting my father killed, but I still miss him. He was my first kiss and for a while he was my closest friend. I thought I loved him. Sometimes."

"Sure."

"Even though he was a monster."

"Those aren't all mutually exclusive. That's one of the things that makes life hard. I mean, always get rid of monsters, but you're allowed to mourn them, too." He looked me over, as if trying to gauge whether or not his words were sinking in.

"Have you ever been in love?" I asked, my mouth again moving faster than my brain. But, once my brain caught up, I decided not to feel ashamed. It was a fair question. My cheeks burned anyway.

He didn't take offense. "I've had my share of crushes, but I never courted anyone when I was human. I was pretty shy."

"Really?"

He nodded. "And the supernatural, ah... appearance enhancement happens to angels too. I was pretty average looking."

"I know how that goes. I'm guessing angels don't date, though."

I expected him to laugh and shake his head, but instead he hesitated.

"We can fall in love," he admitted. "There are members of the order who were married when they were mortal, and they stay together eternally. There are members who fall in love after both have ascended. We wouldn't be able to do our work if we lost our capacity to love."

"Is that why you said I shouldn't let go of falling in love or feel ashamed of what happened with Evan?"

He nodded. "Love is the source of good," he said. "The longer I live, the more I believe that. Kindness, charity, benevolence, those are all variations of love."

I thought about Evan. "Love may be the source of good," I said. "But stupid teenage infatuation isn't."

"Well, you don't learn anything without practice. You're allowed to get things wrong sometimes, and you, I suspect, are always hard enough on yourself when you get something wrong that you don't need other people harping on that point."

"Harping? Seriously? I've got an angel telling me about harping?"

He chuckled. "It's the only harping I know how to do. Just being honest."

"I'm so disappointed."

His smile was genuine. There wasn't any other way to describe it. He really did find me funny.

My nausea was gone, at least. The rest of my feelings about Evan would take far longer to sort out. "Where do we go now?" I asked.

"Back to school?" he suggested. "Darissa usually plays the long game, so odds are she won't make another move for a while. Maybe next week at the earliest. Time moves differently for an immortal and she likes to toy with people and wait long periods of time to get them to let their guard down. But I'll watch over you, of course. No matter how long it takes."

"Okay, yeah. I'd like to go to school." Classes and fearing for my life would also help distract me from the guilt of having murdered someone. That was not a thought I ever expected to have pass through my mind.

He looked me in the eye to make sure I was serious, then put the car in gear.

DESPITE ALL THE excitement of the morning, I was back in class by the middle of third period, Corban shadowing me. He didn't follow me around the whole time. Rather, he slipped in and out of my classes and patrolled the hallways. I assumed after centuries of fighting with Darissa, he knew what he was doing.

Amy was in my third-period class, so after the bell rang she came over to find out where I'd been that morning. "It's a long story," I said. "I promise I'll tell it later."

Between fourth and fifth period, I ducked into the bathroom, and since it was empty, I took my time washing my hands and putting on some lip gloss.

Someone cleared their throat behind me, and I looked up to see who it was. Only, there was no one standing behind me.

Then again… I was looking in the mirror.

Ice shot through my veins as I turned around and found myself face to face with a girl who looked about my age. She had long, black hair with green streaks in it, and a cruel smile that said she was very, very happy to have caught me unawares.

28

"Liana, isn't it?" the girl asked me. "I don't believe we've met. I'm Darissa." She held out a hand.

I went for my phone but she grabbed my wrist, spun me around, and pinned me against the mirror, then fished my phone out of my pocket herself. My shoulder popped from the way she'd wrenched it, and I felt the cool glass of the mirror against my cheek and the back of my arm. Any attempt I made to break free or even push against her hurt like sunrise. She had me in a joint lock of some kind.

Corban was near, though. It was only a matter of time before he found me and it occurred to me that my fear would help him have the element of surprise. Any sensible person would be terrified right now, so if I went into a gibbering panic, I could tell myself it was all part of the plan, really.

"Now, now," she said, putting my phone in her pocket. "No need to call lover boy."

Was she talking about Evan, or did she know about Corban? *Evan*, I thought. It had to be Evan.

My knowledge that decapitation and sunlight could kill a vamp was useless, given I couldn't so much as scratch her with my fingernails. Buffy the Vampire Slayer I was not.

Darissa leaned in close and sniffed me.

Okay, that was weird.

"So it's true. You're only half turned."

I wasn't sure if she expected a reply, but I hoped not giving her one was some kind of assertion of power. Or was it acquiescing to her power? Why oh why hadn't I figured out that being a nerdy recluse would rob me of so many practical skills? I think I'd had some silly conceit that I was watching humanity from afar, when I'd actually spent my time afar reading textbooks and ignoring humanity.

"I'll make you a deal," she said. "You let me study you, and I let you live."

Now that I hadn't expected. "What?" I managed to gasp.

"Specifically, you let me study how it is you survive sunrise." She let go of me.

I collapsed into a heap, smacking my shoulder on the sink on the way down. It wasn't a terribly dignified moment, but I was well used to this kind of humiliation at this point in my life. Boarding-school hazings had prepared me.

She stood over me, eying me down her aquiline nose. "I've heard of your kind, but never one that lived more than a day. Even those, I've only heard of second and third hand." She flipped her hair back over her shoulder. "Do we have a deal?"

Since I couldn't think fast enough to respond immediately, I merely looked up at her in terror.

To say her appearance surprised me was an understatement. She had dyed hair and vampish beauty in the form of flawless, slightly olive skin and piercing gray-green eyes, but she didn't have much in the way of fashion sense. Maybe she was in disguise, but she wore a plain, rumpled t-shirt that showed a beige bra strap. Vampirism seemed more like a red or black bra kind of condition. Her jeans were ill fitting and bagged and sagged oddly, though her waist was plenty slim, and she wore hiking boots on her feet.

Hiking boots.

I supposed those would help her if she'd been chased around the desert by Corban, but again, vampirism seemed like a stiletto-heel kind of condition. Even a proud nerd like me never dressed this frumpily.

Darissa, I realized, was a kind of vampire I'd never imagined existed: a hard-core nerd-girl vamp.

Her glare down at me wasn't all cold derision. There was uncertainty in her stance, too, and the longer she let me wait before I replied, the more leverage I realized I had. The fact that she'd moved this quickly to nab me was another clue. She wasn't making threats or posturing. In fact, it was clear that she *really* wanted to research me, and once I'd picked up my badly scattered wits, it was obvious why.

"You won't be able to use what I do to survive sunrise," I said.

Then I cursed myself. How many times had I mocked movie villains for monologuing their plans, only to do the same thing?

When I was pinned down, no less! I had exactly one thing she wanted, and I'd told her that it was worthless.

Fortunately, she didn't believe me. "I can't?" she asked. "Because I'm not pure in heart like you? I'm not a good person deserving of keeping my immortal soul?" She spoke mockingly. "Maybe that kind of superstition works for you, sweetie, but I'm more of a rational empiricist."

Of all the insults anyone could have hurled at me, claiming to be more of a rational empiricist than I was had to be the worst. It *stung*.

And she wasn't finished. "Not that I expect you to understand what I'm saying, but it would appear from my research that a vampire is a human in symbiosis. A transfer of both blood and saliva from another vampire gives you two different biological agents that together take over the human body like a virus, but not quite. Viruses use RNA to make cells manufacture more of the virus. The vampiric symbionts reprogram the cells to make them immortal, but they also impart extreme photosensitivity and an altered metabolism. The only food source that will work is fresh human blood, which might be plentiful, but comes with a social stigma. Sorry, was that too many big words for you?"

I made myself take a deep breath and debated whether or not to get to my feet. Sitting on the floor, she could tower over me with her hands on her hips, but she also couldn't knock me down again. Given that, I stayed where I was.

Besides, she was doing the villain monologue thing now, so I needed to listen.

"Now you," said Darissa, tapping her ragged, chewed fingernail against her bottom lip, "you seem to have found a way to have your human biology reassert itself without killing off all of the symbionts. They seem to retreat into reservoirs in your system and start multiplying again once the sun goes down. It seems to me that all I'd need to do is to devise some sort of treatment that knocks the symbionts back a bit while allowing the human cells to regenerate, and any vampire would be able to do what you do."

"Are you a biologist?" That didn't fit with the image I'd had of an ageless manipulator.

"I have a doctorate from MIT in biochemistry," she said, lifting one perfectly formed eyebrow. "And a doctorate from Cambridge in microbiology. A medical degree from Stanford, and another one from Oxford, but that was a few hundred years ago. I like to redo my training every century or so in medicine. I have degrees from universities that humanity doesn't even remember existed."

"And they all offered night school?" I quipped.

Her smile conveyed genuine respect. "No. Many of them didn't even admit women. I attended by proxy, shall we say? Found a willing man to go to the necessary lectures and classes but I did the work." She tilted her head to one side. "Does the idea of being able to be an eternal student appeal to you?"

I had to admit, it did.

"Well, well," she said. "Evan said you were a nerd, but I have a rather high bar as far as that goes. You might just clear it. Listen, if you let me research you, I will find a way for you to live forever without having to do the bloodsucking thing. We'll find out how to let you walk around in the sunlight and live off food, like a human, but live long enough to get as many degrees as you want."

That sounded way too good to be true, but she'd also stopped glaring down at me in such a threatening way. I'd read in a book once that the way to get out of a hostage situation was to keep the person talking.

Here, I thought I might actually be able to do the thing the book said. It wasn't like I had a shortage of questions. I selected one that would elicit the kind of information Corban and his order would want to know. "How old are you?"

With an arrogant smile, she sat down cross-legged in front of me. "I was born a Nabatean," she said. "Now impress me. Tell me you know who we were."

Yesss! I thought. I could play this game. "The builders of Petra. In Jordan." I'd visited those ruins one summer with my father; the most famous was the great counting house, a columned facade carved right into a cliff face, its entry leading into a cave.

"Okay, I'm impressed. I'm roughly Corban's age, give or take."

My blood ran cold again. How did she know Corban was around if he was invisible to her?

Her mouth curved into a smile. "I've been eavesdropping around the school. He doesn't change his name often enough. And he's not terribly smart. The principal had his name written down in some notes about him being a narc or something?"

I had to get her to change the subject, but how?

It was time to go full nerd and hope that baited her. "How does a symbiont allow you to go into mist form?"

Her eyes brightened. "That's an interesting one, isn't it? You ever seen the YouTube video of someone putting a sea sponge through a screen? Cutting it into a zillion little pieces and having it re-form again on the other side?"

"No," I said. "But I have watched the documentary that clip probably comes from."

She inclined her head, as if to say, "Touché." "Mist form seems to be an even more advanced form of that. Biology is capable of all kinds of things that look magical to a more... primitive mind."

I got the distinct impression she was calling me one of those primitive minds, and I resolved not to care. Which wasn't to say that was easy. I'd endured all kinds of insults in my life, but they were all about me being too nerdy. It rubbed me raw to be told I wasn't nerdy enough. *Stay calm*, I ordered myself.

"So," I said, "don't you think turning into mist form requires the symbionts to alter your DNA to an extent that they can't be extracted or, knocked back, as you say?"

"Well, you have many of the physical changes that the symbionts provide and you can still survive sunrise. You've got the vampy prettiness, at least. Do these questions mean we have a deal?"

No, no, I thought. I had to keep her talking.

29

Darissa's lips curled in a triumphant smile.

"Do we have a deal?" I repeated. "I don't know about that…"

"Oh, let me guess," she said in a pouty tone. "You're mad at me because I killed your father."

Now that was a gut punch. That void that Corban had left in me when he absorbed my guilt flooded full to the brim. She had killed my father. Because I'd been stupid and let a guy turn me into a vampire, she had hunted down my father and shot him with a sniper rifle through his window. He'd never stood a chance.

"Well," she said, "here's the deal, sweetheart, I can kill your aunt, your friends Gina and Amy, anyone who looks twice at you. We can do this the easy way or the hard way. It's up to you, because I will get what I want either way."

Okay, she was evil all right. Nerd or not, she would never have my respect.

"Or," she said, "you're mad at me because I haven't even asked about Evan? That I consider him expendable? That's what happens to people who cross me. They become expendable. Did you kill him last night or is he hiding somewhere because you broke his heart? You know what? I don't care."

Right, so she had the full, stereotypical villain playbook. Great.

But right then, the bathroom door swung open and Corban stepped in.

And my intense look of relief gave him away.

Darissa leapt to her feet, and from the way her eyes weren't focused, I gathered she couldn't see exactly where he was. Corban wasn't invisible. Like he said, he was being overlooked.

"I think that's enough," he said, calling attention to himself so that she could see him. "Liana, get out and make sure no one else gets in." He held open the door.

I tried to dash for it, but Darissa was faster and stronger. One second I was getting to my feet, the next I was down with my head ringing like I'd been swatted up the side of it with a frying pan. My nose felt numb and when I touched it, my fingers came away sticky with blood.

But I didn't have time to wallow in my pain. Corban was down. Darissa had him on the floor and was straddling him, her hands around his throat, skin touching skin.

He wasn't choking so much as fading, getting visibly weaker while she continued to squeeze.

I cast about for a way to save him. I could knock Darissa aside, but she moved with superspeed and Corban, to my knowledge, didn't.

To the left of me was a bloodied brick lying on the floor. The doorstop, I suspected. Darissa had grabbed it and smacked me with it. Bricks were good for that sort of thing. I looked towards the far wall, at the high windows that were painted over with opaque paint, blocking out all sunlight.

There was a chance that they weren't painted glass, but rather sheet metal or plywood or something that wouldn't shatter when I threw a brick at it, so as I threw I also lunged for Darissa to knock her off Corban.

Never had glass breaking sounded so beautiful, so perfect.

Corban heaved himself up into a squat and something flashed in his hand. He held it against his wrist so that I couldn't see it well, but I suspected it was a short, needle-like knife that could slip between the ribs and into the heart. Now that seemed much cleverer than a stake.

He didn't get a chance to use it, though. Darissa had poofed into mist and poured her way down the drain in the tile floor. She left my phone behind and I snatched it up before grabbing Corban by the collar of his jacket and dragging him towards the door. I didn't want to risk staying in the dim sunlight of the bathroom. We needed real, full sunlight that Darissa definitely couldn't endure.

He spun, grabbed my arm, where it was covered by the fabric of my jacket, and pulled himself to his feet. The two of us stumbled out the door of the bathroom, which I would have expected to cause everyone walking past in the hallway to turn around and gawk at us, but no one did.

"Corban," I said. "Conserve your energy. I don't care if people see us and laugh at me."

But he was still fading fast, nearly passing out on his feet. I wrapped his arm around my shoulders, put my arm around his waist, and managed to get him outside into the fresh, cold air. We both collapsed against the school building.

His breathing was shallow and he groaned as he leaned back.

I wished I had a habit of carrying food in my pockets, but I didn't. In desperation I went through his pockets and came up with a granola bar. I peeled back the wrapper and gave it to him. "Eat," I said. "Get your strength back. I've got all kinds of fear from what just happened. You can have it."

He bit off a corner and chewed slowly, and the terror that had been making my heart pound slipped away.

"Are you all right?" I asked, feeling my own nose. It didn't seem to be broken, and I managed to staunch the bleeding with a tissue from my pocket.

He took a deep breath, then nodded. "Thanks to you, yeah."

"How is Darissa able to make her clothes go into mist form with the rest of her? Why did my phone stay behind? Does she have a phone?"

His eyelids fluttered open and he looked sidelong at me. "Really? After what just happened, that's what you care about?"

"It's weird. I don't get how–"

"Liana, in case you haven't figured this out yet, I am not a scientist. I have no idea. Why? Do you see some way to use that against her?"

"No…" I confessed.

He started to laugh, a chuckle at first that built into a real laugh.

"I was just wondering," I said.

But that only made him laugh harder. If he hadn't nearly died moments ago, I would have slugged him with my bare hand. I couldn't pack much of a punch, but my skin would have stung him a little.

As it was, I had to sit there with my knees pulled up against my chest and glower at him.

"You're unbelievable," he said. "Liana Linacre, you're one of the nerdiest people I've ever met. Ever. In millennia."

"Hey!" I snapped. "Come on."

But he was laughing so hard that he was sliding down the wall, about to roll on the ground.

I looked away from him and waited for him to finish.

Which took far too long.

By now people had started to notice us. Nobody gaped openly, but people gave us plenty of side-eye as they walked in and out of the door beside us. Or maybe they only saw me, sitting alone with an angry look on my face. I had no way to know.

When the last of his guffaws finally did fade, he rolled towards me and nudged me in the side. "Thank you," he said. "You were amazing in there."

"How could you let her almost kill you?" I snapped.

"I miscalculated. I always do with her. She's fast, even for a vampire, and she always figures out how to get me off balance. I was planning to sneak in and surprise her, but then I heard her threatening you and I got mad and… fine. Be mad at me."

"You've been around for how long?" I asked. "And you almost threw it all away for one strange… specimen like me?" Even with my careful word choice, I hoped no one overheard me. I'd have a lot of explaining to do if they did.

"Okay, calm down."

"Don't tell me to calm down."

"Fine, I'm sorry." He held up his hands. "But it turned out okay. I'm okay, you're okay. I suggest you go get yourself excused from the rest of the day at school. Darissa's stuck in the storm drain, and there aren't many places that she can get out without getting burned. She's gonna have to sit under the school while the sun's out, which means we have until sundown to make another plan."

"Like what? To use mirrors to illuminate the whole storm drain with sunlight?"

"We'll figure something out. But first, I'm still hungry, and not even all the teen angst in Taos is enough to replenish me. Let's go."

30

I would not let Corban make me drive while it was full daylight and there was traffic on the road, so he did get behind the wheel, but his reflexes were impaired and he wasn't able to drive the speed limit.

Fortunately, this was Taos. Creeping along slowly attracted plenty of honks, but didn't stand out enough for anyone to call the police. Since he was clearly out of it and I didn't know where else to go, I directed him to the burger joint.

In the middle of the day, it had customers, but we found a booth in the corner, away from everyone else, where I deposited Corban, then went to get him a hamburger, fries, and soda. I got the same for myself.

He blinked when I dumped his in front of him. "Thanks."

I slid into my seat and unwrapped my hamburger.

He took his time opening his, moving as if every joint and muscle ached. I emptied some ketchup packets onto a napkin for his fries and put the straw in his soda.

"Thanks," he repeated, taking a bite of his burger.

"Is this place good feeding?" I asked. "Is there enough pain around here for you?"

"In a minimum-wage establishment next to low-income housing? Yeah." Already the color was returning to his face.

"So what's your plan?" I demanded. "Please tell me you have something better than running at her with a sharp object?"

He chewed, swallowed, and gave me a somewhat sullen look. "Every time I've planned ahead, she outplans me. If I go spur of the moment, she can outfight me. I may be stronger, but she studies enough combat styles that she can outfight nearly anyone. I told you, Darissa is hard. Okay? We'll work together."

"I'm not *that* smart," I said. I was fighting the urge to yell at him. It just didn't seem right that he couldn't put together a better plan. This, I realized, was the reality of fighting a very old, immortal being. They could continue to get smarter and stronger indefinitely. "How many centuries have you zoned out while she was studying?" I asked.

The look he shot me conveyed real hurt.

"Sorry," I said.

"Fighting vamps is not my main job," he said.

"No, you're right. I'm sorry."

"But in case you haven't figured it out. In case she didn't make it clear to you, I'm a back-of-the-class, dumb-jock kind of a guy."

"No, you're not. I really am sorry, okay?"

"Yes, I am. Some of us, even with eternity, do not become these brilliant shining stars–"

"Corban," I said, "I did not mean to insult you. It was my fear talking, all right? I take it back."

He said nothing, just ate and watched me. He still seemed weak, though I couldn't put my finger on how he showed it. His posture was straight again, but he seemed more fragile and less substantial.

That made me nervous. "You're going to recover by nightfall, right?"

"I don't know."

"How bad did she hurt you?"

He rubbed his throat. "Her skin's a lot more tainted than yours."

For a moment I wondered how that worked. Whether he had symbionts that could be hurt by hers, and then I realized now was not the time for pointless nerdery.

"How do you recover from her, then?" I asked.

"I could use a nap."

"Okay. You sleep?"

"Not usually, but I don't usually eat either. When I'm beat up I do."

"How long do you sleep? Like, hours, or decades or–"

"Uh," he said with a wry smile, "my landlord would definitely get suspicious if I went decades. I'm hoping an hour or two tops."

"Okay… so your place? Or is Cassie's house safer?"

"We've put Cassie through enough for one day. And yes, my apartment is warded against Darissa. My kind has our own protection spell, but if you want to cut your toenails, too, I can probably find some clippers."

I rolled my eyes and he laughed.

At least we had somewhere safe to go for the rest of the day.

"Darissa's systematically killed most of the scholars in my order," he said. "We've stolen copies of most of her research, but she's hamstrung us. We used to have a team always coming up with new ways to fight vampires. Nowadays, we have to improvise more."

That explained why Darissa seemed to know exactly as much about half-turned vamps as Corban did.

"You're low on nerd angels?" I asked.

"Fortunately, no. We're living in a pretty nerdy era, so we've had quite a few ascend. Darissa goes after the oldest ones, though, so all of our scholars are youngsters. Less than a century old. They can read old research, but they didn't do the research. It gives her an edge. At least, that's what I understand the issue to be. Which isn't saying much, I know."

"You're not stupid," I said. "I would zone out if I had to do high school for two thousand years too."

"I don't have to do high school," he pointed out. "I do it because I blend in and because I care about people in transition to adulthood. I feel like I know a thing or two about that. And yeah, a lot of problems I see are repeats. Just because it's repetitive for me, though, doesn't make it less important for every single person who goes through it. I keep doing it because I care. People at the end of childhood are vulnerable in ways that impact the rest of their lives, and I will help every single person I can. That will never bore me."

I stopped chewing for a moment. Corban's talk earlier about the importance of love snapped into focus. Or at least it became clear to me that he knew things about love that were well beyond my mortal understanding. My temptation to study for eternity now felt shallow and small beside his eternal life's work. "I'm sorry I insulted you."

He shrugged. "You were freaked out. You thought I was going to rely on you to come up with a plan to deal with Darissa and you just saw her own me."

"Well... yeah." My mind was tacking off elsewhere, though. A new pang had formed in my chest.

"We can try to outsmart her," said Corban, "and if that doesn't work, we can find another way to get her to leave you alone. We can frame your death or something. We can call other members of my order. Time is on our side."

As I saw it, time was neutral and would benefit Darissa as much as it did Corban. But again, now was not the time to be pointlessly nerdy.

He watched me closely, then reached out and grasped my forearm over the sleeve of my jacket. "Hey, you all right?"

I looked down at his fingers wrapped around my arm and he let go, pulling back with uncertain slowness. "What's wrong?" he asked. "Besides both of us blowing up a prairie dog town and then getting attacked by an immortal demon this morning?"

I smiled because I didn't want to drag us both down with the sudden turn in my mood. What was wrong, though, was that it had stung to hear him talk about how he loved everyone. Every time I spoke to him, I knew how much he cared about me. There were times, like this morning, when he made me feel like I was the only person who mattered, but that was because he was good at loving people, not because I was special.

It reminded me of a conversation I'd had with my dad. "Your mom was my best friend," he'd confided to me when I was still a little kid. "I don't see myself getting married again because it's rare to find a friendship like that. She got me, and she loved me anyway."

For a week after that conversation I'd been paranoid that my dad would hate me, given my mother had died from complications in childbirth, but he'd seen my unease and sat me down for another talk. When I told him that fear, he'd smiled and said, "Your mother didn't tell anyone about her blood-clotting condition because she was afraid doctors would tell her to terminate her pregnancy. She was too soft-hearted to risk hearing that. The thing about me and your mother is that I got her too. I understood how she thought, and I can't be mad at her for loving you more than herself. That was part of what made her the amazing person she was."

In my delusion all those nights with Evan, I'd thought that he loved me like that because he tolerated my nerdiness. Maybe he'd even had a thing for nerds, if Darissa was anything to go by. Now I was sitting across from a guy who literally did love me for who I was, without exceptions.

"Liana?" asked Corban.

"We're friends, right?" I said.

"Sure," he replied, still watching me closely.

"Just friends?" I regretted the words as soon as they were out of my mouth.

31

This literal angel, seated across from me at the burger joint, was so much older than me that his age could almost be measured in geologic time. To say he'd think I was immature was an understatement.

But he was also old enough to know how to handle my awkwardness. He folded his hands, relaxed his shoulders, and said, "Well no. You saved my life."

"Right."

"And I admire you. I respect you. You've done things I didn't know were possible."

But… I thought. I knew there was a "but" coming and I stared down at my half-eaten burger and waited for that shoe to drop.

Except, he stopped talking. When I looked up, he returned my gaze with a wistful smile. I got the impression that he was like an old man watching a shooting star, because if I was mortal, my life would be over that fast for him. But he was going to watch until the streak of light faded.

And he wasn't laughing at me, or rolling his eyes at my feelings.

As the moment stretched on, I found that for once I didn't mind being stared at by an attractive guy I'd fallen for. I didn't worry about dumping my drink down my front or saying something stupid, because he didn't need me to say or do anything. All he expected was for me to be me.

It wasn't his fault or mine that the barrier between us was insurmountable. He couldn't be the love of my life, but he could help me learn how to exist without apology. I didn't think it was something I could pull off anywhere or anytime else. Not yet, at least, but here in this moment with him, I could, and I tried to accept that as enough, because it was all he could offer.

I bit my lip, then took a sip of my drink. Looking down at my half-eaten hamburger had also shown me that I'd been eating it all this time without tasting it. What was the point of eating junk food if I didn't at least enjoy the taste?

Corban resumed eating his fries.

I finished my burger and fries and sipped my soda until it was gone, him waiting patiently all the while. Then we gathered our trash, threw it away, and headed out the door.

CORBAN'S APARTMENT WAS in the small complex that Gina had shown me before. It was tucked between a strip mall and some single-family housing.

I had to help him up the stairs and through his door and into a pretty regular-looking studio apartment, roughly the size of my dorm room at the Hawke Academy.

A futon couch was pushed against one wall, and he had a television and stereo system. A kitchenette at one end was equipped with a small fridge and a couple of burners. I suspected he didn't care about limited fridge space and no oven; he spent his time snacking on the pain of the people around him.

I helped him convert his futon so that he could lay down with his back to me, facing the wall. The only other place to sit was on a beanbag chair in the corner, and I flopped down on it.

"Hey, Corban?" I asked.

"Mmm?" he replied.

"How many of your kind are there?"

"I dunno. A lot. I'm the only one out here, but in Santa Fe there are at least five. Albuquerque has, like, fifty. Denver's got hundreds. We've been around a long time, and we're adding members faster than we're losing them. We're probably the most common form of altered human."

"The most common form?"

"Mmm-hmmm. Vamps used to be second. They often are second, but not right now."

"So what other forms are there?"

He chuckled. "Trust me, that is a much longer conversation." His words were beginning to slur, though, and his breaths to deepen. He was slipping into unconsciousness.

Which left me alone in his apartment.

I CHANGED MY mind a million times in the hours that followed. I even did all my homework, completing an essay that wouldn't be due for a week, as if that mattered right now. Teachers always thought I was hardworking, when I suspect the truth was that I used schoolwork as a way to escape from life. It was something my mind could do on autopilot while time ticked by.

But Corban stayed out cold for one hour, then two, then five, then seven, and that drove me to the inevitable conclusion that he could not face Darissa again before sundown. If he was going to face her again, he'd do it after he recovered. I realized that might also be after I was out of the picture.

Because I decided I was going to kill her or die trying, and I was fully aware that the latter was more likely. It still made sense, in the grand scheme of things, for me to try.

Corban's kind might be common, but they were also needed. I might be a novelty, but at the end of the day, I was just another vampire.

I paced his apartment and laid out the facts in my mind as best I could. The first thing I had to accept was that I was not as smart as Darissa, nor was I a better fighter. Nor was I interesting enough to distract her for long.

There were only two things I had going for me: the fact that I was interesting enough to distract her for a short time, with my novel half-turned-ness, and the fact that she didn't know me at all. She probably knew enough about people and fighting them that I wouldn't be able to surprise her, but there was a miniscule possibility that I could.

I finished this thought process standing over Corban's sleeping form and took a good, long look at his face. We had known each other for exactly one week, and he'd been gone for most of it. It was strange how many memories were crammed into that time, though.

My one regret was that I knew he'd be upset about my decision, but I nevertheless believed he'd understand it, and after being asleep this long, he would expect it.

And he'd get over it. He'd go back to his predictable existence, helping thousands upon thousands of other people step over the threshold from childhood to adulthood and easing their burdens along the way. Even if I was a really, really good investment banker, I wouldn't ever accomplish anything like that.

Cassie would be upset, too, but Corban would help her cope.

A thousand years from now, when he was still around and I was a hazy memory on the brink of fading forever, details like whether I'd lived to eighteen or eighty wouldn't matter. Whether Darissa survived this day, however, would.

Corban's jacket was draped over the arm of the futon, so I was able to get his keys from his pocket and slip out, locking the door behind me.

The sun was setting, and I wondered if I'd be able to get into the school. I didn't suppose that mattered much. Darissa would find me, I was sure.

It felt truly weird to drive without Corban in the passenger seat, and I did feel bad about stealing his car, but my mind kept going to the grand scheme of things. It just didn't matter all that much.

The school parking lot was mostly empty; only a few teachers' cars winked their reflectors at me as the RAV4's headlights swept across the lot. I did my best to park and then debated over what to do with the keys. I finally decided to leave them in the car and leave the car unlocked. Either Corban would get his car back, or someone would get lucky. (Though unless that someone was from out of town and could leave fast, Corban would still get his car back.)

The school proved to be unlocked. Had they learned nothing from the attempt to burn down the library? There were still staff members around, though. I saw some lights glowing through classroom doors and heard the distant sound of footsteps on the tile.

I tiptoed, even though I supposed that was unnecessary, back to the same bathroom where Darissa had almost killed Corban, and pushed open the door. More light spilled into the dark hallway and I had to squint a moment.

She was there, waiting for me, examining her nails as if she was the sort of person who got manicures, and she took her time lifting her gaze to meet mine. Her smile was triumphant.

"Sooo, you here to take the deal?" she asked.

"Yeah," I said. "I am."

32

Darissa took me out the back door of the school, across the sports fields, and to a car parked on one of the residential streets.

A very nice car. A Corvette.

"Don't damage the leather upholstery," she said as she unlocked it with a click of the key fob.

I sat down and buckled myself in, which she found amusing, and we were off. Unsurprisingly, she drove like a maniac. Like an immortal who wasn't bound by small concerns like speeding tickets or having to kill a cop to get out of one.

I gripped the door handle and kept my head down as she sped out of town in a direction I'd never been before. By process of elimination, I surmised we were headed to Taos Ski Valley, since we weren't going to the pueblo, my aunt's subdivision, or Santa Fe. First, though, we raced across the Taos Valley floor, blowing through a little town that went past in a flash.

"So what do you plan to do with eternity?" she asked.

"I figure I'll have some time to decide." My knuckles were going white.

"True."

"I've been accepted at Princeton."

"A good school," she said. "I've studied engineering there. By proxy." She winked at me.

Keeping her eyes on the road was something else she didn't really bother with. At least not until a minute or so later when we started up a steep mountain road.

Once again, all my knowledge came from the internet, but I knew that the ski valley was its own little village up closer to the peaks, at the base of all the chair lifts and such. It was only in business in the winter and was a ghost town in the summer.

Aunt Cassie had also told me of some extreme Earthships that I would be able to see out the left side of the car on the way. "Those are completely off-grid, with radio telephones," she told me, as if I was supposed to know what the heck a radio telephone was. I was feeling too woozy to look out the left side of the car though, as that was where the drop-off was to the valley floor below. I focused on the road and on not thinking about what I was about to do. I hoped she hadn't learned yet how Evan had died. If anyone had gossiped in the bathroom about an explosion out by the Earthships, she would probably figure it out.

Every now and then I glanced at the rearview mirror, wondering if there were headlights behind us. I didn't know whether to hope for them or not. I didn't want Corban to rescue me, but the romantic in me nevertheless wished he'd try. That was foolish, but it was also human, and I was getting to like being human.

Corban was smart enough to play the long game, and his stupid antics that morning would no doubt remind him of the fact. No, I was on my own, which was what I wanted. Really.

Up and up we sped, taking curves so fast that I was developing a bruise on my hip where my seat belt buckle dug in. Well, that would make Darissa happy, seeing that I could bruise.

"So, the nice thing about the urgent care center in the ski valley," said Darissa, conversationally, as if she wasn't driving seventy miles an hour up a winding mountain road, as if our mutual ex-boyfriend hadn't been offed earlier that day, as if we were just two friends on a fun ride. "The nice thing about their urgent care is that it's only open while the lifts are running. It closed at four, and the last patients were out of there by five. I figured you'd appreciate me waiting until the place is empty?" She glanced over at me.

"Sure," I said.

She cackled, which was so stereotypical I almost rolled my eyes. But I didn't want to overplay my hand. I was unique to her, but she was immortal. I still ran the risk of her deciding that I wasn't worth her trouble. It was best to stay meek.

A scattering of lights up ahead was the ski valley, I decided. Only it wasn't. We blew right on past those, taking a ninety degree turn so fast that I was surprised the car didn't go up on two wheels.

"Arroyo Seco," she told me. "The most common town name in New Mexico, and also the home of Taos Cow Ice Cream."

"Cool," I managed to say, even though I was not thrilled at having to go up even more mountain switchbacks at breakneck speed.

I wondered if I ought to keep talking to her, like this was a hostage situation, but then I also thought that I shouldn't make it obvious that I felt like I had very little time left to be alive. I needed to behave as if I expected to live for centuries.

The ground outside was turning white, which meant we were entering the snowcap. The road was still clear; rocks and grains of sand pounded against the sides of the car as we barrelled on.

More lights up ahead were, I fervently hoped, Taos Ski Valley. Fortunately, this time I was right. We blew past the sign proclaiming it as such without slowing down, and the lights proved to be lodges and hotels built on the steep sides of the mountain.

Darissa took a right turn so fast that we narrowly missed a Range Rover that honked at us angrily.

"The nice thing about heading to a medical facility," she said, "is that people forgive you for speeding." We screeched to a stop in front of a little strip mall. The urgent care center had glass doors that showed that it was indeed closed; the lights were off.

Darissa strode purposefully up to the door and unlocked it, winking at me as she did.

I looked away and didn't bother to wonder whether she'd just stolen the key or killed its owner and then stolen it. The air up here was downright frigid. She pushed me inside the antiseptic-infused interior and locked the door behind us.

"So," she said, "the equipment here will do for now. I've devised other tests that we can run later, when we're back at my own lab. One thing about living forever, you learn that humanity is always forgetting stuff. If you guys kept better records, you'd probably have FTL drives by now. You'd at least have the kind of testing equipment I've been able to assemble." Her boots squeaked on the tile as she took me back to an exam room. Only there did she turn on a light.

So she did care about getting caught. A little, at least. And her unique lab meant she had a reason to keep me alive past tonight.

"Sit, sit," she said, pointing to the exam table.

I climbed up on the table and sat, the butcher paper used to cover it crinkling under me. She left for a moment and returned with a needle and some vials.

"Do you care which arm?" she asked, holding the needle up.

I extended my right arm. "Better blood vessels on my dominant side," I said. This was a random fact that a woman interested in my dad for a few years had told me. She was a physician who had appreciated how I hung on her every word. Dad had liked her as a friend; he hadn't really bothered to date. My eyes were stinging at the memory of him; I quickly blinked the tears away.

"True," said Darissa. She fluttered her eyelashes at me as she wrapped the rubber tie around my upper arm and cinched it up tight. With a pensive frown, she inspected my inner elbow, poking and prodding until she lost patience and resorted to smacking the flats of her fingers against my skin to get a vein to rise.

"Aside from a blood draw," I said, "what else are you going to do?"

"Cheek swab," she said. "And then we take another set at around midnight, blood draw and cheek swab, and then another right before sunrise, and another right after."

That all made sense. She'd probably look at the levels of symbionts in all the samples and maybe even be able to see how much they'd altered any of my cells from the cheek swabs.

"Would a regular doctor notice anything in my blood draw?" I asked.

"I have no idea," she said, lining the needle up with my vein. "I know what to look for, but I don't really pay attention to what you call modern medicine. Though I suppose vampires have gone in for blood draws before, or to donate blood, thinking they can steal blood bags. It does them no good, of course. I think the anticoagulant used to store human blood neutralizes any nutritional value, and they probably end up killing whoever tries to stick them with a needle. Ready?"

Before I could react, she slipped the needle into my vein and taped it down, then put the first vial in place.

Deep-red blood welled up inside it and she waited until the vial was full before swapping it out for another. She shook the full vial to distribute the anticoagulant, then set it aside.

She took four vials in all, then slipped the needle out of my arm, slapped on a band-aid, and stepped out of the room.

A moment later she was back with a swab and a petri dish. "Open wide," she said.

I did and she took a sample from the inside of my cheek.

"O-kay," she said, her voice sing-song because she was upbeat. I was being her perfect patient, and we were about to make medical history. Real medical history, apparently, without the risk of merely rediscovering something humanity had forgotten after some past, apocalyptic event that wiped out whatever society had recorded it.

Though I supposed what we were truly making was hidden history. Real history might not ever know anything about her research, unless she succeeded and turned most of humanity into sunlight-walking vampires.

She needed to not succeed, and I needed to not get too nervous. She'd smell my nerves and likely get suspicious.

"How are we getting back to your lab?" I asked.

"There's a red-eye flight," she said. "Albuquerque to... well... I suppose it doesn't matter where." She waggled her finger in my face, tsking me.

I sat back, not caring.

"You want some dinner?" she asked.

I hadn't eaten anything since that hamburger, and it made sense to fuel up, but at the same time, I felt like time was running out. There was only one thing I came here to do.

Headlights lit up the hallway outside as a car pulled up to park. Darissa didn't react, didn't peer out into the lobby area or anything.

No, I thought. *No, no, no.* Corban had caught up with me. It had to be him. Somehow he'd tracked me here, and I couldn't imagine how. Well… unless there were enough people along the route freaked out by Darissa's driving to leave a trail. I couldn't risk him trying another rescue attempt.

The memory of my run through downtown Taos last night was fresh in my mind. I hadn't lost my soul immediately then. I could turn vamp and still control my actions for a little while according to the dictates of my human conscience. The key was to act fast.

Darissa had her back to me, but I knew she was aware of me and I was sure I now stank of fear. It was best to assume she knew I was about to do something, and she was waiting for my move.

Here went nothing.

I stared at my hand, then unfocused my eyes, willing it to dissolve. The shift in my body was immediate and almost painful. The smell of my own blood in the nearby glass vials was suddenly pungent, and the incandescent light brightened so that the room was lit up like midday.

But I pushed all that aside and reached for Darissa.

She spun around, eyes wide with horror. "No!" she squeaked as she saw my hand and arm dissolve into mist form.

Someone opened the front door and stepped into the front lobby.

I got off the table and stepped up to her, sending the tendrils of myself up her nose, forcing myself to watch so that I did it right. Up her nose, and then down her throat. Decapitation killed vampires, and Evan's death had given me an idea.

She inhaled in surprise, which pulled my mist tendrils deeper. Her eyes conveyed utter bafflement. I had caught her offguard.

It was time to strike. *Try not to think of sleeping prairie dogs when you do this,* I told myself.

I raised what was left of my arm, and snapped it back into corporeal form. For a split second nothing happened. Crushing pressure on my hand and forearm hurt so bad that my vision began to gray out.

Then all at once, Darissa's head, neck, and part of her chest ruptured, bursting outward, towards me. My tendrils had gone deeper than I realized.

I ducked back, expecting to get splattered with blood and gore, but she didn't explode like a human under pressure. She poofed into dust, erupting like a cloud of ash from a volcano and dissipating.

And just like that, Darissa was gone, leaving only dust that hung in the air and made little piles on the floor. I noticed that I didn't cough. That was because I didn't breathe. I'd turned fully vampire. My human soul would soon be winging away from me while my memories shifted over to a demon.

I made a point of not dusting off my clothes. That seemed vain and vampy. Instead I took in the scene around me. I tried to make myself understand that I'd just killed a mastermind. Against all odds, I'd won.

I'd *won.* My gamble had worked. I might be about to die, but it was worth it. I was leaving the world a better place than I'd found it.

I'd have to make myself content with that.

With all the dust on the floor, it appeared that Hollywood had gotten something right after all, though I squatted down to inspect the largest pile to make sure it wasn't just some altered version of mist form she'd entered to fool me.

"Dammit!" Corban shouted, bursting into the room and sending the dust swirling and dancing across the floor. He reached for me.

I winced back from his touch. "Don't," I said. "It's too late. It's done." My stomach began to growl something awful and there were several vials of blood in the lab that smelled better than a freshly seared steak, tender and juicy. I wanted to eat them, glass and all, even though I knew they wouldn't do anything for me.

No, I thought. I forced myself to stand, and stay still, just like I'd forced myself to stay in the sunlight for sunrise. "Did you just swear?" I asked him.

He didn't laugh this time, though. He looked at me with tears welling up in his eyes. "Liana."

"It's done," I said. "Darissa's dead. It was worth it, okay? There are billions of other humans on the planet. One of them will end up half-turned like I was, sooner or later."

He shook his head and put his hands on my shoulders, then placed one on the side of my head, my hair protecting him from contact with my skin, his eyes looking into mine.

"I need your help." I said. "I need you to kill me, or at the very least, make sure I face sunrise." The world was getting faint as I spoke. The final transition was coming now. My soul was leaving my body. "Promise me?" I begged.

I don't know if he did. The world went dark before I got an answer.

33

I felt like I was floating, and like someone was slowly peeling my skin off. It felt like sunrise, almost. Was this death?

From the pain came an awareness of my body, how I lay prone and suspended. Someone had a hand braced against my chest.

More pain, like a thousand knives slicing my skin, and then the familiar sensation of molten metal and my body swelling up like a blister. This was definitely sunrise.

I began to move, and the hand on my chest held me down, or under actually.

I was being held underwater, I realized, as I tried to thrash my arms. The pain kept building and I felt the water around me get warm and start to bubble. I didn't feel like I needed to breathe, either. That was bad. I set my jaw and opened my eyes, feeling the sting of water right up against my eyeballs and able to see nothing more than a dark field above me. I had a hazy impression of someone standing next to me in the water, still holding me down.

The pain was getting more acute and my field of vision began to turn a blinding shade of white. I forced my muscles to go slack. If this was how I died, then so be it.

Water churned around me as the pressure on my chest shifted. The person ducked down underwater with me and had his arms around my waist. It was Corban. I knew his touch. A hand cupped my cheek, and he pressed his lips to mine.

No, I thought. This would kill him.

I brought my hands up to his chest, intent on pushing him away, only his response was to hold me closer and deepen the kiss. I found myself clutching the front of his shirt. Water was boiling around us, or so it sounded like, but he weighed me down, like an anchor, and kissed me like he'd been waiting for the chance for centuries.

My arms went around his neck, my fingers raking through his wet hair. The pain in my body burst, but I stayed intact. A sensation like a cleansing pulse went through me, and the water around me, originating from his kiss.

I finally managed to get my hands against his chest again, and this time I did push, tearing myself away from him. I bobbed up in the water, my face breaking the surface as I gasped down a deep breath of air. The air was full of steam, but the water was only warm, not boiling hot.

My eyelids fluttered open and for a confused moment I looked around. I was in Cassie's studio. My mind slowly pieced together that I was squatting in the pond at the bottom of that infernal waterfall.

And Corban was slumped over in the water, face down.

I panicked and threw my arms around his torso, hauling him up out of the water and heaving him towards the edge. A wave sloshed over the lip of the pond and spread across the floor of the studio, but I managed to get Corban's upper body to follow it so that he lay on his back, head lolling, so I had to cushion it with one hand to prevent him from cracking his skull. He lay half out of the water, gasping and coughing. I wrestled him onto his side so that he'd be able to expel any water he had in his lungs.

He coughed and heaved while I backed away across the pond. I didn't want to risk touching his wet clothes, in case the wetness prevented them from being a barrier to my tainted skin.

Slowly he got his arms under him and hauled himself the rest of the way out.

"Corban?" I said.

He was still too busy coughing up water to reply.

I climbed out of the pond and pressed a finger to my throat. I had a pulse, all right. I was breathing. I was human once more; full immersion had prevented me from burning up in the sunrise.

But wait, I thought, *how had Corban gotten me into the house when I was a vampire?*

I looked up at the stairs, and there saw my aunt in that stupid bathrobe of hers, standing anxiously, wringing her hands.

"You," I said. "I told you not to invite me–"

"That's drinking water, you know," she cut me off. "I hope you're ready to pay for a delivery from the water truck. I'm going to have to drain the whole system."

"Um... fine," I said.

"And don't tell me who I can and can't invite in my own house," she snapped. "It's my house." She turned on her heel and stomped her way up the stairs. A moment later, the front door slammed.

Next to me, Corban began to chuckle.

I looked down at him, relieved that he had come around, and his eyes were open. There was something about his eyes, though. They were the same shade of blue, but they weren't quite as ethereal.

I watched as he put two fingers to his own throat, his mouth quirking in his signature, wry smile.

"What?" I asked.

He reached out and put his hand over mine.

I pulled back, but he sat up and did it again.

"It doesn't hurt," he said. He flopped back down on the floor. "It doesn't hurt."

Then he passed out.

I MUST HAVE passed out too, because the next thing I remember was waking up in my own bed, the late morning sun streaming in through my window and the house dead silent. All I wore was my underwear and bathrobe.

In the kitchen, scrawled on a scrap of paper, was a note from Cassie. "Liana, I've checked myself into a facility for a couple of days. I've got my phone with me. Gina brought over your tamales and offered to drive you to school this morning. I told her you were sick, and I've called you in absent today. I'm really, really sorry if it seems like I'm abandoning you. It was all just a bit much. -Cassie."

A bit much? That was an understatement. I managed to locate my now damp clothing, draped over the shower door downstairs. The floor of Cassie's studio was dry, but the waterfall was turned off. No wonder the house was so silent.

I called Corban.

"Hello?" answered a male voice that wasn't Corban. "Is this Liana? Liana Linacre?" The man spoke with a deep timbre and a clipped accent that made me think he was from sub-Saharan Africa.

"I'm trying to reach Corban."

"Yes, yes. We've been expecting your call. How are you feeling?"

"Sorry, who is this?"

"My name's Michael."

"You part of Corban's order?" I asked.

"Yes. We–"

"Where's Corban?" It was all I could do not to burst into tears.

"Recovering. He's okay, but he needs to recover."

"Can I speak to him?"

"Not now, no. Not now. We want to speak to you. To run some tests on you. Would that be all right?"

"Tests?"

He was quiet for a moment, then said, "Ms. Linacre, I am very sorry about what you had to endure without support from the order. Corban felt he couldn't tell us about your situation and get our help, and I fear he was right. But now you've proven yourself to be something quite different than a regular vampire. Several of us find that intriguing."

"I want to talk to Corban," I said. "Not to be rude, but I don't know who you are and Corban saved my life."

Another pause, then, "I'll see what I can do. Please be patient, all right?"

Well, I wasn't in any mood to be patient. According to my phone it was just after ten, and there was no way I wanted to stick around the empty house with no homework to do and nothing to distract me. The problem was that I had no way to get to school, unless Taos had Uber. I downloaded the app in desperation and was pleasantly surprised. They did.

So I sent for one and did what I always did to escape, I went to school. I got a ride with a cheery woman who had harp music blaring on her radio and I noted on my way past that some SUVs and people wearing what looked like park-ranger uniforms were tending to the blown-up prairie dog town. I couldn't bear to look to see if they were handling limp prairie dogs.

I went to class, then ate lunch with Gina and Amy, telling them only that I hadn't been feeling well and that I had "a few things to deal with from my dad's murder." It wasn't a lie.

And I didn't withhold the information from them because I was pushing them away. They were both my new touchstones of normalcy, and I clung to that. I listened to Amy mutter about her brother's lack of ambition and Gina's wistful wishes about starting her own jewelry line. It felt so *good* to be the boring one who just ate and listened.

The cafeteria served shepherd's pie that day, and I'd been distraught that it would be too much like other mundane cafeteria food. Then I saw people dumping green chile on it and tried a little myself–much less than what the rest of the cafeteria considered a normal amount. Even the little bit I used made my eyes water, but it also made the shepherd's pie a lot less boring. I was getting wise to the New Mexican way of making all food better with chile.

In art class I actually felt inspired for the first time, though the art teacher at the end of the period gave me a diplomatic critique that let me know that art was more than inspiration. Still, she was really nice about it.

After school I went home with Gina to help her with homework, not that she needed it. She was more scared of failing than she was in danger of failing. While I walked her through a math problem my phone rang, and Corban's number popped up.

Gina didn't bat an eye when I excused myself and went into the bathroom with my phone.

"Hello?"

"Hey…" Corban's voice.

"Hey!"

"So, yeah, sorry we all abandoned you."

"Who's 'we all?'"

"Erm… about fifteen members of my order were in your house after I lost my powers."

"Lost your powers?"

"Yeah, I'm human now. It's probably temporary. The order's sending me on some other assignments while I recover my abilities."

"Oh." I let that sink in. "Is that bad? Did I hurt you?"

His voice gave away nothing, not that it ever did. Had he meant it when he kissed me? Or had he just been desperate to save the most novel vampire he'd ever met?

"It's not bad that I lost my powers, no. It's more evidence that I was right about you. A vampire should have been able to kill me with a kiss. You're different, and the order wants to be able to study you a little. They won't do anything without your consent, and they'll share whatever findings they have with you. I warned them that you'd probably understand the data better than they will." Even when he mentioned our kiss, he talked right on past it.

And I was still processing what he said about being human now. "So, wait, what happened to you?" I asked.

"I overtaxed myself. My abilities are like a battery and I'll have to recharge for a while."

"Oh… How do you do that?"

"I keep doing my work, minus the feeding for a while. Don't worry about me, all right? I regret nothing."

I clutched my phone, frustrated that this was the only way I had to speak to him. I wanted him here, in person. "Where are you?" I asked.

"Turkey."

That word hit me like a wet, slushy snowball. I'd assumed he was still somewhere nearby, or at least in the country. I assumed that I'd be able to pressure him into seeing me face to face. Turkey was half a world away. "What?" was all I could manage to say.

"I'll probably be working at some refugee camps here for a while," he said.

Working in Turkey? Not here in Taos? "Wait… will I ever see you again?"

Silence.

A tear formed and slid down my cheek.

"Liana, you've got a life to live. A regular, normal, mortal life, which is already going to be a tall order with everything you've endured so far."

More tears followed the first. "What does that have to do with seeing you again?"

"I will never, ever forget you, okay? Not if I live to be a million years old."

There were good-byes and then there was this. I inhaled and it sounded like a sob. It was a sob.

"Hey," said Corban. "You're going to be okay, I promise. My kind all know who you are now. You're never gonna be left alone again. You're a hero."

If I'd learned anything in the past few months, it was that life was full of situations far too big for me to change or control, and they flew at me fast whether I was ready or not.

All I could control was how I handled each one. This, I now realized, was probably the last time I'd ever speak to Corban, and there just wasn't time for me to waste arguing about it. I took a few deep breaths and gathered my wits as best I could. "Thank you," I said, "for saving my life. Like, multiple times."

"It was a privilege."

"And… umm…" I was crying in earnest now. "Can I see you at least one more time before I die? Even if it's, like, fifty years from now?"

"If it's in my power, then yes."

"You've gone rogue from your order before," I snapped. "And they forgave it."

He cracked up, laughing like he had so many times before at the things I said that I hadn't meant to be funny. "Yeah, all right. I'll see you someday, Liana Linacre. You take care of yourself and have a good life."

I whispered my good-bye and heard the line cut out.

"Liana?" Gina was at the bathroom door. "You okay?"

I took another deep breath, and it came out as another sob. "Yeah," I still managed to say. "Really sad about some stuff, but… yeah… I'll be okay."

To Be Continued...

ACKNOWLEDGEMENTS

I owe a lot of people some heartfelt thank yous. First thanks always goes to Dr. Char Peery—my beta-reader who must like me a lot to still be doing this after so many years. We met as housemates in 2002 and I haven't managed to make her throw a manuscript at my head yet.

My critique group, Critical Mass, helped me draft this from beginning to end. They are: S.M. Stirling, Lauren C. Teffeau, John Jos. Miller, Sarena Ulibarri, M. T. Reiten, S.E. Burr, and Rebecca Roanhorse.

My editor was Sally Gwylan, a talented author in her own right (check out her short stories if you get the chance.)

And a massive thank you to all the ARC readers on my mailing list who caught lingering typos. They include: Susan Niedermeyer, Sharon Bass, Pat Johnston, Patricia Duffel, Chrisna Booysen, Jerry Millett, Annette Sly, Ivy Liu, Viola Braxmaier, Rebecca Evans, Jeff and Jessica Ney-Grimm, and several others who prefer not to be named.

Those ARC readers and my ebook formatter had to deal with the buggiest file ever. We could not figure out what had messed it up so badly. Stacey Tippetts, however, is a master and managed to fix it to make a beautiful ebook. Tara Jones did the paperback (and Tianne Samson rounds out the formatting team.) The cover layout and that awesome title block were done by Linda Caldwell.

Finally, I need to thank my boys for tolerating a mommy who is always at her computer, and my husband for putting up with me muttering about the plots of every movie and television show we watch. My guys are the best!

Made in the USA
Middletown, DE
06 May 2019